Mary Powley

Echoes of Old Cumberland

Poems and translations

Mary Powley

Echoes of Old Cumberland
Poems and translations

ISBN/EAN: 9783337398248

Printed in Europe, USA, Canada, Australia, Japan

Cover: Foto ©Andreas Hilbeck / pixelio.de

More available books at **www.hansebooks.com**

ECHOES

OF

OLD CUMBERLAND.

POEMS AND TRANSLATIONS.

BY

MARY POWLEY.

LONDON: BEMROSE & SONS.
CARLISLE: G. & T. COWARD.

MDCCCLXXV.

P R E F A C E.

THIS Volume is inscribed to the People of Cumberland and of Westmorland, to whom it may be of most interest; in the hope that the endeavour to preserve a picture of local scenes, and in either County, a record of habits and customs which are passing away from us, will be a better apology for its publication, than the request of friends; or the wish that these, the recreations of many years, may entitle the Writer to a kind remembrance.

Several of the earlier Pieces have appeared many years ago, in local Periodicals; others more lately, anonymously, except in one instance. Many left unfinished for years, are given with trifling additions, and nearly in the order of their composition. Some were written to preserve in remembrance, and in their proper connection, expressive old words which seemed then in danger of being lost; because they belong to a district less fortunate in collectors and illustrators than the North or West of Cumberland. And explanations are offered of such words, or allusions, as may render the sense less generally intelligible. A date with a title indicates the time to which the description refers; a date at the foot, is that of composition.

LANGWATHBY,
March, 1875.

CONTENTS.

	PAGE
Address to Cross-Fell	1
A Mother's Influence	7
Memory and Grief	13
Kilspindie ; or, The King's Revenge	16
Langanbye	24
The Gleaner	31
Brough Hill before Railroads	35
"And this also shall pass away"	41
Solon	44
Easter Day in Country Churches in Cumberland	47
The Petrified Forest, near Grand Cairo	50
The Pass of the Icebergs	54
On an Ancient Grave	59
Invocation to Patience	64
England, the Meadow Land	67
The Woman of Mind. A Parody	71
To Penrith Beacon	75

vi.

	PAGE
Friends	81
To the Pack-Horse Bell of Hartside	85
The Dove	92
The Moor—Enclosed	94
Eden	98
To the Steam-Plough in Caithness	100
To my Purple Beeches	102
Summer	105
A Tale of late October	108
The Funeral Psalm	112
The Heaf on the Fell	114
Eden's Story	120
Waiting for the Day	125
The Last Tree of Inglewood Forest	127
The Welcome East-Wind	132
An Incident of Emigration	134

	PAGE
DIALECT	135
Difference of Opinion about our Mudder Tongue	139
"I niver rued but yence"	143
Cumberland Thanksgiving Song	145
The Brokken Statesman	148
"To see oursels as ithers see us"	152

	PAGE
TRANSLATIONS	154
Elsinore (Danish)	155
Tycho Brahe's Farewell do.	158

vii.

		PAGE
Uranienborg	(Danish) -	161
The Thorn Hedge	do. -	166
Jutland	do. -	167
Zealand	do. -	170
Langeland	do. -	172
Home-Longing	do. -	177
Fatherland's Song	do. -	181
Soro	do. -	183
Frederiksborg	do. -	186
The Broken Ray	do. -	189
Evening Song	do. -	191
Northern Song	do. -	194
On Mœn's Rock	do. -	197
Spring Song	do. -	201
The Smithy of Heligoland	do. -	203
Holger Danske	do. -	207
Sœren Nordby	do. -	214
The Danish Soldier	do. -	218
Monument and Boundary Stone	do. -	223
Sœborg	do. -	225
The Grave-Digger	(German) -	228
Alexander Ypsilanti, at Munkacs	do. -	231
My Wish	do. -	234
The Grave in Busento	do. -	238

Relph. 1712—1743 - - - - - 241

ADDRESS TO CROSS-FELL.

CROSS-FELL! Confederate of the storm,
    Grey monarch of the mountain range!
    Calmly for ever towers thy form
  Above this atmosphere of change;
And ever, as our footsteps turn,
Seems watching o'er their homeward bourne.

Though fells our bleak horizon close,
  And hills o'er hills above us peer;
To thee alone our valley owes
  Tribute of dread, O, mount austere!
And notes thy signs of gloom or grace
As subjects watch their tyrant's face.

Thou treasurest up the streaky snows,
  In wintry thrift pre-eminent,
And oft where Spring's soft verdure glows,
  In lowly vales, thy blasts are sent.
And when the harvest-time is near,
Thy menace puts the land in fear.

1

Oft wild winds break their shadowy band,
  And through the vales thy storm-voice thrills,
And shivering—foodless—patient—stand
  " The cattle on a thousand hills ; "
While hissing sleet, or hurtling hail
Are downward driven upon the gale.

Old prostrate trees and scattered corn,
  Spring-showers of leaves, like Autumn's, shed ;
And severed branches, tempest-borne,
  And drifted snow, o'er pit-falls spread.
The withered herb, the roofless cot,—
Can thy storm-trophies be forgot ?

Yet, wizard fell ! while o'er the land
  From thy veiled brow the shadows lour,
Oft have we climbed the height, to stand
  Within the circle of thy power.
And almost with our childhood's wonder,
List to its dread continuous thunder.

Our earliest vision met thy form,
  Old Atlas of the Eastern sky !
Our ear in childhood knew the storm,
  Whose billowy voice roared wild on high,
And where those mighty winds were furled
Seemed then the boundary of the world.

We love thy smiles, as children love
    Th' unbending of their warrior sire ;
And e'en thy hostile panoply
    And helm, by fancy's light admire ;
And climb thy skirts, or clutch thy crown,
Without the fear to meet thy frown.

Rise, veteran blast ! unshorn in power,
    With memory's fragrance on thy wings ;
Thy fierce assault—thy deafening roar—
    The garb that, fluttering, closer clings,—
Not sweetest gales of Araby,
Could bring such precious spells to me.

Our Pagan fathers wond'ring stood
    As rose, 'mid calm thy tempest's wrath ;
Or when their stalwart strength was bowed
    As some fierce whirlwind barred their path ;
While reigned around mysterious gloom,
And far was heard its thunder-boom.

They dreamed of wild unearthly forms,
    Haunting thy lone and lofty brow ;
Pouring their demon-rage in storms
    Upon the western vales below.
And when thy orient helm appeared,
The present fiend our fathers feared.

Dark ages passed : and on our land
　　The Day-spring from the east arose ;
And holy men, a zealous band,
　　God's word to demon might oppose ;*
And raise the Christian standard here,
With rite of exorcism, and prayer.

How beautiful, on this stern pile,
　　The feet of him of old who sought,
And to our lone and desert isle
　　Glad tidings of Redemption brought !
And here, perchance, we press the sod
Those apostolic feet have trod.

Thy slopes are green, thy cloudless brow
　　Where winds the sheep's, or shepherd's path,
Retains nor saintly traces now,
　　Nor vestige of the demon's wrath ;
And whether reared of wood or stone,
Augustine's cross, can ne'er be known.

* A local legendary tradition ascribes the expulsion of the
Demons of the storms from "the Fiends' Fell," to Augustine
and his forty followers, who, in the course of their missionary
labours in these parts, erected upon the hill in question, a
cross, from which it is said since to have been called Cross-
Fell.—See *Hodgson's Northumberland.*

And since those men of days remote,
  O, wild and seldom-trodden fell !
Shepherds alone thy heights have sought,
  And thou hast kept thy secrets well.
Though, fain Philosophy would trace,
Thy howling Helm-wind's nursing place.

Save that in long, bright summer days,
  When springs are low, and winds are still,
And Nature's pilgrims climb, to gaze
  From each lone peak, and lofty hill ;
Glad troops of friends have often tried,
Who first should scale thy slippery side.

And oft the sheep, below that seem
  Like stars in heaven, or ships at sea,
Stirless—apart—as in a dream,
  Images of tranquillity ;
Fly their lone spring and tender grass,
While troops of laughing gypsies pass.

And seldom shall the young and fair,
  E'en where earth's varied beauties meet,
Find loveliness that may compare
  With the bright scene around thy feet,
O'er which the gathered spells of time
Have cast their witchery sublime.

NOTE.

Cross-fell is the highest point of that range which the Romans called Alpes Penine—sometimes called by courtesy the British Appenines, and in more homely language "the back-bone of England." This chain extends from near the Scottish Border (dividing Cumberland from Northumberland, and Westmorland from Yorkshire,) into the heart of the kingdom. The Helm-wind peculiar to this fell has been the subject of much discussion, but philosophers are not yet agreed as to its causes, or rather, as to the manner of their operation. This wind often rises when the sky is clear and the atmosphere perfectly calm, but it is always preceded by a white cloud over the summit of Cross-fell, fancifully called "the Helm." In a few minutes this cloud may have extended itself over the entire outline of the fells for the space of five or six miles north and south of Cross-fell: a gloom seems to hang over the country, and the wind blows from the east—often with tremendous fury, and a sublime roar, resembling that of a stormy sea. The Helm-wind prevails frequently during the spring months, and much retards vegetation in the vales immediately below Cross-fell; and its influence is felt, though its force is proportionally mitigated, at a distance of six or eight miles. Nine days is held to be the usual period of its continuance at one time.

A MOTHER'S INFLUENCE.

"Train up a child in the way he should go ; and when he
is old he will not depart from it."—SOLOMON.

A Mother's influence ! what can bound
Its wide extent, its depth profound?
On Life's parched track, though lost to view,
Its power survives ; as morning dew
To herbs supplies, 'neath summer's sway,
Strength to endure the fervid day.
E'en in those hours of soft repose
The infant pilgrim dimly knows,
When angel-whispers light the smile
That brightens o'er its face the while.
As poets sing,—might love not deem
Its mother's image prompts the dream?
Some dim mysterious consciousness
Of kindred love and watchfulness.
Ever at hand to soothe, to bless?
And with the faint perceptive ray
That brightens into Reason's day,
Through childhood's careless sunny hours,
Its life of glee, its path of flowers.

The Christian Mother's influence
Shall link with each awakening sense,
That greets with wonder, awe, or love,
The opening world, a world above ;
By thousand apt analogies,
In Wisdom's path that daily rise.
That Power Supreme, whose word "Be light !"
Kindled that sun so wondrous bright—
Each morn recalls ; each fading day,
When rises many a fainter ray :
The roving moon, and far and lone,
Stars ever changeless, shining on.
E'en outer darkness, childhood's dread,
When beauty to its sense, seems dead ;
Save by the hearth which brightly burns,
Save in those eyes to which it turns.
That Power that caused the streams to flow,
Taught trees to wave, and flowers to blow,
Which gives to all of life the breath,
Resumes the gift. and this is—Death.
That Mercy whose regard divine
On little children deigned to shine,
Who blessed, and bade them all draw near,
And still their lisping prayers will hear ;
That Justice whose all-seeing eye
A little child's deceit can spy,—
Are linked in thought, a precious store,
With childhood's ne'er forgotten lore ;
With birds and flowers and all things bright,
Springs of its ever fresh delight ;

With all familiar things, or strange ;
With Time's, and Youth's, and Seasons' change.
  So fall a Mother's accents bland,
So rears and twines her skilful hand,
While flexile yet, with tender ease
The heart's soft sensibilities.
With many an amaranthine flower,
With stems of firm perenniel power ;
Or sows 'neath vernal skies of youth,
In human plots of genial mould,
Seed that may yield a thousand fold
Of bright and heaven-aspiring Truth.
  Those days are o'er—the youth departs
From home's pure joys, and loving hearts ;
But first, he strays, with lingering sadness,
Through many a scene of childish gladness ;
Winds with the brook, his playmate oft,
Through many a dell and flowery croft,
Where, idly angling, he would pass
The truant hours ; or on the grass,
In summer's sunshine wont to bask,
Conning some lesson—scarce a task ;
Or with his brothers, in their glee,
Half drowned the wild brook's melody,
Or 'mid its brawling current played,
Or slept beneath its hazel-shade :
Lingers in bowers his sisters loved,
And alleys where, their sport, he roved,
In long bright days, amid the flowers :
A memory for life's darkest hours.

The walks his mother loved to tread,
And where his tottering steps she led,
And spoke those words, whose echoes still
The chambers of his soul shall fill.
The hearth her gentle eye illumed,
When fireside joys most sweetly bloomed ;
And where, his father's cares unbended,
The sire was with the playmate blended ;
That hearth where he was wont to glean,
At social wisdom's feast serene ;
And where the Sacred Word was taught,
And youth was trained to solemn thought.
He views with lingering filial glance
His native landscape's wide expanse ;
But dares not lift his eyes to trace
The parting grief on each loved face ;
Yet struggling rebel tears belie
His outward show of apathy.
But in the light which hope bestows,
He silent parts—and forth he goes,
With man's resolve—the world to brave ;
And, by the might of blessings poured,
And grace, by fervent prayer implored,
The world shall ne'er his soul enslave !
   Oh, happy youth ! the favoured heir
Of earth's least earthly love and care !
No chequered lot, no distant clime,
Nor gold, nor grief, nor gnawing time,
Shall disunite the links thus tied
By her, his spirit's faithful guide.

Nature's fair face is ever fraught
With holy harmonies she taught.
Summer's deep noon, in leafy bower,
And moonlight's solemn softening power;
And twilight's calm, but social gloom,
When thought o'er vanished scenes will roam:
Those hours restore, in lands afar,
The form that was his childhood's star;
And though that form in death be still—
And dark those eyes love once did fill,
Its influence is ever bright,
Her smile is with him in *the right;*
Is beaming to confirm—assure
In whatsoever things are pure;
Restraining might is in her tears,
A chastening woe her image wears,
When folly tempts, or sin would blot
The purity of early thought.
Was all for this—the vigils kept,
The tears shed o'er him while he slept,
Her heavenly hopes, and earthly fears,
Her living love, and dying prayers?
No! still that hallowed memory,
Through all vicissitudes, shall be
Unto her child, in after time,
An amulet 'gainst woe or crime.

O'er the low tombstone, graven deep,
Rank weeds and russet lichens creep,
And yet though sore defaced to view,
Beneath, th' inscription still is true.

So characters, by love first traced,
E'en Time's rough hand hath not effaced ;
His Mother's image ne'er shall part ;
Her monument is in his *heart*.
O'ergrown and gray with worldly cares,
Cumbered with twining hopes and fears ;
Yet when Mortality shall clear
From earthly stains the record there ;
Beneath th' accumulated heap,
None shall be found so true, so deep ;
His closing tomb reflects the ray,
That o'er his cradle wont to play.
And faith, and peace the world ne'er gave,
Of its dark terrors rob the grave.
　　But, lightly o'er his ashes tread,
Whose steps no pious Mother led :
Upon whose spirit's gloomy dawn
No load-star of affection shone,
To guide his soul to Mercy's throne.
Uncheer'd oft, by such hope or aid,
Through Life's dark maze he downward strayed,
And guilt and woe, with fearful weight,
His dismal doom accelerate ;
Nor radiant hope, nor heavenward trust,
　　May check the tears that kindred shed
　　For him—the lost—the early dead—
Like that which beams above the dust,
And cheers the mourners of the just.

MEMORY AND GRIEF.

Our Northern Sires, unskilled in Art,
  But in the might of Nature strong ;
Of iron frame, and earnest heart,
  Full rudely poured their thoughts along,
Yet aptly wont, of old to name
Remembrance, Thought and Grief the same.*

As summer's lightest breeze steals by,
  The thistles' down its course will show ;
As scents reveal where violets lie ;
  Or, footprints, wanderers in the snow.
And so this word, at random caught,
  Seems but the echo of a thought.

These men of Odin's creed of blood,
  The troublers of the olden time,
Of desperate valour—stern of mood—
  War their religion—peace a crime,—
Had then the lore with years we buy,
They knew that "memory is a sigh."

* The same Saxon word, *mænan*, which means to express
grief, means also "to think," to remember.

The strife and death their warriors sought,
  Their pageants, conquests—Fame retains;
And of their inner life and lot,
  This trace in Northern speech remains.
And now, a vision o'er me steals,
Of old heart-griefs this word reveals.

Such breasts in human mould were cast,
  Of human woes endured the smart;
And, haply, pondering o'er the past,
  A poet's, or a woman's heart,
With insight deep, and utterance brief,
First linked together Thought and Grief.

Or, some gaunt warrior, left to wait
  In age and impotence, the grave;
Whose sons had reached, through slaughter's gate,
  The high Valhalla of the Brave,
Unconscious of its two-fold chain,
Might so have breathed his spirit's pain.

Stern Death, where kindred ties entwined,
  As now, then severed—partings wrung—
Falsehood betrayed—and Love declined—
  Hopes faded—and Disease unstrung
The harp in whose sad quivering tone
Sorrow and Memory were one.

Ages have passed.   And though we scorn
  The rude and uncouth Saxon tongue;
And deem of riper time is born
  This thought—the theme of many a song;
No later poetry can reach
Beyond this Gothic truth of speech.

And all that ages since have taught,
  Of varied terms—of polished Art,
Have failed to sever in our thought,
  These old partakers of the heart;
And Truth and Feeling still would name
Remembrance and Regret the same.

An After-Thought.

Yet, lingerer o'er thy fancies sad !
  Find'st thou not joy in memory too ?
Mercies and gifts to make thee glad,
  Such as thy fathers never knew ?
And heedless—thankless, would'st thou name
The Christian's thought and grief the same ?

KILSPINDIE;
OR, THE KING'S REVENGE.

A HISTORICAL BALLAD.

The following ballad refers to that period of Scottish history during which James V. exercised such unrelenting severity, and so effectually humbled the pride of his nobles ; among whom, those of the house of Douglas in particular felt his revenge, for their ambitious encroachments on the royal privileges, and for the personal restraints imposed on himself during his minority, by the head of their house, the Earl of Angus.

In Scotia's stormy days of yore,
When civil discord ragèd sore,
  And chiefs their king defied ;
And Douglas, crafty, stern, and bold,
Beyond his sovereign's power, controlled
  The eastern border wide.

King James, like a furious steed, no more
Will brook the curb of his noble's power,
  Nor a subject's thrall will be :
Angus is hurled from his pride of place,
And banishment to all his race
  Is the monarch's stern decree.

As his native hills in the storm stood fast,
As Tantallon's towers repelled the blast,
　So the haughty Angus stood ;
And long, when the gathering cry was heard
Of "Douglas"—as weak was the monarch's word,
　As his who would bind the flood.

And fierce and dark waxed the royal gloom,
With the earl's resistance to his doom,
　Which fraud at last o'ercame.
But an oath the fiery monarch swore—
" Henceforth, no Douglas serves us more !"—
　And he sternly kept the same.

.　　　.　　.　　.　　.

Bright shone the sun on Stirling's towers ;
His beams had dried, in its pleasaunce bowers
　The dews of morning sheen.
The royal pile seemed throned in air,
Beneath lay the valley wide and fair,
And the Forth wound, brightly devious, there,
　As loth to leave the scene.

The forest wore its brightest shades ;
The deer were browsing in the glades
　Of Stirling's sylvan park ;
All round was Nature's richest grace.
And where the sun declined his race,
In contrast strong, the eye might trace
　Benlomond's outline dark.

2

And, nursed 'mid Campsie's southern hills,
Came their bright meed of sparkling rills,
  To swell the widening Forth ;
Far east, Dun Edin's towers were seen,
And, sweeping round, the Grampian screen
  Fenc'd out the chilling north.

And the king and his nobles from hunting passed,
With sylvan pomp and bugle blast,
  With a proud earth-shaking tread.
O, who could dream of woe or care
In that pageant gay, that scene so fair ?
That passions dark were monarchs there,
  And its living bloom o'erspread ?

Yet one with fainting step and slow,
With wrinkled brow, and locks of snow,
  Comes o'er the green expanse ;
His foreign weeds bear many a stain,
And he seems to writhe with inward pain,
As he halts to see the gorgeous train
  To Stirling's pile advance.

Kilspindie, of the Douglas race,
Renowned for courtesy and grace,
  In his monarch's sports had shared,
And the king in boyhood loved him well ;
Of his manly feats each knight could tell,
Ere the lightning stroke on Douglas fell,
  That none of his name had spared.

And now, long years of exile past,
The grey-haired man had come at last,
  By a desperate impulse led,
To sue for his sovereign's clemency—
To die, if such his will might be ;
But again, whate'er the penalty,
  His own loved hills to tread.

And oft from his lip pleased murmurs came,
And his eye seemed lit with youthful flame,
  As it fell on the vale beneath ;
No foreign scene had claimed such glance,
Nor streams had seemed, in sunny France,
So bright as those which ever dance
  Round his native hills of heath.

His home-sick sense had lightly scanned
The fairest scenes in the southern land,
  In whose wars his blood he had poured.
And he knew how proudly the warrior dares,
For his native land, and the name he bears,
Compared with him who bravely wears
  A mercenary sword.

And as with his form remembrance woke,
" Ho !—yonder is my Greysteil ! " broke
  From the lips of the gallant king.*

* "Archibald Douglas, of Kilspindie, was placed by the
Earl of Angus about the person of the king, who when a boy
loved him much for his expertness in manly exercises, and
was wont to call him his Greysteil, from the name of a
champion of chivalry in the romance of Sir Eger and Sir
Grime."—*Godscroft.*

That sound of the past seemed eloquent;
But the flash is not more quickly spent,
That through ocean's treasure caves is sent,
  By the lightning's gleaming wing.

Had the name his boyish sport conferred
No fresh and kindly feelings stirred?
  Nor could the king recall,
How oft in his boyhood's wayward hour
That name was a spell of enlivening power;—
As the shepherd's strains, when clouds would lour
  O'er the darkened mind of Saul?

Or lives the bard, though thrice a king,
Whose memory doth not fondest cling
  To the friends and the sports of old?
If such love in King James' heart had place,
It was choked by hate of the Douglas race;
For he made no sign, nor slacked his pace,—
  And his glance was stern and cold.

As the aged man knelt down in his path,
And strove to turn away his wrath;
  And with an exile's agony,
Whose heart the worst of woes had braved,
A life obscure and lone he craved,
  Or a grave in Scotland free.

But the iron-hearted king rode on,
Stern and unanswering to the tone
  Once dear,—but now wild and hoarse ;
As, " Pardon ! gracious king !" he cried,
" Thy scourge hath humbled the Douglas pride !
Let thy wrath on his blood no more abide—
  From his name remove thy curse.

" I bring not the arm of might which served
My king, from whom my heart ne'er swerved
  In dire calamity,—
And if now that heart could falsehood dare,
This nerveless arm no part would bear,
  Against thy realm or thee.

" Oh, sire ! if thy native land is dear,
If the plaint of misery pain thine ear,
  Remit this fearful doom !
'Neath the tempest that another sowed,
My heart is withered, my strength is bowed,
  And my days draw near the tomb !

" All earthly hopes have left my breast,
But my sluggish heart still yearns to rest
  In the lap of my country fair.
Oh, king ! by the memory of days long fled,—
By the blood which my sires for thine have shed,
By the crown of the just on thy royal head,—
  Spurn not an old man's prayer !"

But ever on the proud king went,
Up Stirling's castle-crowned ascent,
 And his steed the faster spurred ;
And the old man kept an equal pace,
Though links of steel his form encase ;—
But his chief of yore here found more grace,
 Who died by his monarch's sword.*

Oh, Chivalry ! it ne'er was thine,
Fetters for age or grief to twine ;
 And thou, the monarch's boast,
'Mid passion's storm was dimmed thy beam,
Which knightly deed and poet's dream
Inspired ; and from his brow the gem
 Of purest ray was lost.†

But, dire Revenge ! we may not know
On guiltless heads, what weight of woe
 Thy frenzied slaves have wrought ;
The usher of Remorse thou art,
The fierce tornado of the heart,
 With desolation fraught.

---

* William, eighth Earl of Douglas, was barbarously murdered in the Castle of Stirling, by James II. ; after having been decoyed thither under the promise of a safe convoy, for the amiable adjustment of his openly avowed hostility to the crown.

† " The brightest jewel in a king's crown is mercy."—
 Proverb.

At the castle gate, like a child subdued,
The toil-worn man sat down, and sued
   For water to quench his thirst.
The tearless warrior's might was frail,
His soul was dark, and his rough cheek pale,
   As died the last hope he had nursed.

But the very menials of his state,
Aping their master's savage hate,
   Refused the meagre dole.
And the old man passed the seas forlorn,
With the iron of his monarch's scorn
   Barbed in his inmost soul.

But the doom which a Douglas might not brook,
And the stain, Death soon from his spirit took;
   And the pangs which deeper rend.
Like his who finds mere sordid dust
Some heart, the shrine of early trust;
Or, who sinks beneath the treacherous thrust
   Of his own familiar friend.

Nor long the unforgiving king
Of revenge the pride,—of remorse the sting,
   On earth remained to feel.
Like the stricken deer who bore his dart,
'Twas said he died of a broken heart!
Perchance he forgot, when he caused the smart,—
   Who strike, shall fall by steel.

LANGANBYE.*

O ! spot of all the land alone,
Unsung, unheard of, and unknown ;
Dim back-ground of life's busy stage,
Scarce named in local history's page.
Neglected spot ! what hast thou done,
That, ever since the world begun,
Thy name proscribed hath seemed to be,
In legend, tale, or minstrelsy ?
That e'en no rustic bard hath owned thee,
And thrown a wreath of song around thee ?
    Alas for thee ! unknown to fame,
Genius hath never breathed thy name ;
And wert thou not, there scarce is one
Would miss or mourn thee, save thine own.
As these wild flowers alone would know
When ceased their parent spring to flow.
And though by all the world forgot,
Yet lonely, dear, neglected spot !
Thy rustic children lightly hold
The world's regard—proud, wide, and cold !

* The popular pronunciation of Langwathby.   Often so
spelt formerly.

The world that bears no thought of thee—
Their loreless souls' mute poetry !
For, mid thy waste, thy verdant hills,—
By thy broad stream, or nameless rills,
Hearts with thy love o'erflowing, beat,
And tuneless lips, afar, repeat
Thy name with fondness, like the glow
That poets sing, or patriots know.
    Loud vaunting Fame, in places high
Proclaims, with fitting eulogy,
Names long unheard, of lowly men,
Never to be forgot again.
But strangers all.   Their glorious birth
Hallows some happier spot of earth :
Of worthies, warriors, sages, bards,
Distinguished by Fame's high awards,
Not one hath lustre shed on thee,
Obscure, ignoble Langanbye !
Neither have chronicles of crime
To tell of thee through distant time,
That one within thy bosom nurst,
Hath died and left his name accurst.
    No spot amid thy hills or plains
Marked scene of ancient deed remains.
And yet thy neighbours of the vale
Have each their legendary tale :
Some tell where Roman legions camped,
And eagles flew, and chargers tramped ;
And, many shared that ridge of green,
That tells where Hadrian's wall hath been.

Some, storied haunted castles hold,
Blent with the fame of chiefs of old ;
Some point to beacon steeps, where blazed
Fires that the country-side oft raised ;
Or, mystic circle on the height,
Scene of some long forgotten rite ;
Or, springs, whence gentle fairies quaffed,
'Neath summer moons, the limpid draught ;—
And yet the spot, green, cool, and fair,
Might well detain them ling'ring there.
But thou ! whom fairy never haunted,
Nor grimmer ghost, or goblin daunted,
No light of giant, seer, or sage,
Reflects on thy dull after-age.
No castle, cave, or Druid spot,—
All but thy name appears forgot.
Yet thou in earlier days hast been
Part dowry of a Scottish queen ;
And more of suffering, more of fame,
I ween, had twined around thy name,
Had not thy bridgeless stream kept ward,
And foes and strangers oft had barred.
That southward track the Scots knew well ;
And Eden's western bank would tell
How hardly with its hamlets fared,
While east, the woe and scath was spared,
Because the Lang Wath lay between,—
Oft sullen floods, of depth unseen.
Easier the Scots by Udford found
To cross the Eamont's narrow bound,

Before its waves in Eden merged,
One swift uncertain current urged,—
To reach the upper valley's charms,
And old Westmeria's richest farms.
    Yet who thy far forgotten prime,
Or listless tale of after-time,
Shall scorn, or deem their lot more blest
Whose deeds historic scrolls attest?
In ancient records ever blaze
The guiltiest deeds, and stormiest days ;
While calm, green, peaceful spots like thee,
Have found no place in History.
    Now fertile fields o'erwrap thy moor,
Once horse-course—battle ground of yore,—
Vague rumour saith.   And late to us
One grave-mound, mute, mysterious,
Showed here some mighty chief had died,
Was laid to rest in warrior pride.
Vain thought !—to pierce the ages' haze,
'Twixt us and those dim olden days.
Or guess what greater things may 'wait
Thy bounds enlarged, thy richer state.
We know, whate'er swift roads may bring,
Whatever future bards may sing ;—
Old Langanbye ! is gone from thee,
That old-world, green tranquillity !

LANGANBYE=LANGWATHBY.

This name has been variously written and explained, perhaps by persons unacquainted with its significance in the simple northern sense of the three words combined*—the village by the long ford—to which all circumstances of the early state of the place point, as the true interpretation. It is certain there was no bridge over the Eden here till the present one, bearing date 1682. It is said in Burn and Nicolson's History of Cumberland that, "the church of this village was probably built for want of a bridge over the Eden, whereby the inhabitants were often prevented repairing to Divine worship at Edenhall." How the church was used while the clergyman was kept on the other side by the frequent floods of those watery times, does not appear ; nor why two parishes on opposite sides of so considerable a stream, so near its confluence with the Eamont, should have been thus united. During wet seasons a west wind often suddenly augments the tribute of the latter, by surplus waters from its great feeder— Ullswater, and causes the lower valley of Eden to be deeply flooded ; formerly with more disastrous consequences, as many persons living remember.

"In the year 1360, the bridge at Salkeld being fallen, Bishop Welton published an indulgence of forty days to all who should contribute to the repair of it."—(Burn and Nicolson, p. 415.)

It may be of this old structure, two miles lower down, that a pile of solid masonry remains in the bed of the Eden ;

* Scandinavian words, of which we have many other forms and combinations. A *wath* is the usual country name for a ford ; *by* is a village.

Has been dug or? by [?...] of Gt Salkeld in the last year. R/P.

it stood upright till a few years ago, when it fell, but is still
to be seen, just above the new railway bridge, near Lazonby.

It is significant that there is no account of Scottish raids in
this parish, while the tenants of Penrith, Great Salkeld, and
Soureby, petitioned the crown in the reign of Edward III.
for compensation for their losses by the Scots, and had privileges allowed in Inglewood Forest.

In the "Agreement between Henry III. King of England,
and Alexander King of Scotland, concerning the lands afterwards called the Queen's Haims"—1237, viz. : "the manors
of Penrith, Soureby, Languethby, Salkild, Carlatton, et
Scotteby," part of 200 librates of land given "in towns where
no castle is situate," in consideration of which Alexander
released Henry from his claims of the three counties of
Northumberland, Cumberland, and Westmorland, &c., which
lands were afterwards forfeited by John Baliol—(see Burn and
Nicolson)—the name is not much varied from the old form ;
but in an enumeration of these lands in 6th Edward I.
"before the King's escheator, Thomas de Normanville"—
Langwaldeofby—looks like an uncertain guess at a meaning,
while Long Waldeofby—if it was so spelt, as Mr. Denton
says, in ancient records—shows only the influence of Norman
French on the language, or the name, but throws no light on
any Waldeof connected with the place at any time, since
Henry I., who gave it with Edenhall to Henry Fitz Swein ;
though it soon reverted to the crown.

In 1745, the Scots did pass over Langwathby Bridge, and
through the village to the moor, and the fell sides. But in
the list of fords to be watched, to oppose the progress of
earlier marauding parties, this name does not appear : it is
possible it might be alluded to by "Ednal and Dolphenby"—
(Udford)—by the latter of which the passage was much easier
into "the bottom of Westmoreland." At a period when ortho-
graphy of names was so much a matter of fancy to those who
wielded a pen. we find that "In 1292 the Prior and Convent
of Carlisle, presented Robert de Scardeburg to the vicarage of

Addingham ; Adam de Crokedayk having also presented
Richard de Longwardby—judgment was afterwards given for
the Prior and Convent.—(Burn and Nicolson, p. 450.)

"In 1376, Sir Richard de Langwathby was presented to
the Rectory of Orton."—(B. & N. p. 208.)

In other old writings and on letters it is spelt Langanbye,
according to its invariable and more convenient pronunciation
in the country. Throughout Burn and Nicolson's History, it
is spelt Langwathby. When or why the change of the first
syllable came in, we have no account ; but long after it was
so taught by the schoolmaster, a good old Vicar used to
resist strenuously, the new spelling and pronunciation ;
always called the village Langanbye and its people Langan-
bians ; nor have any of his successors adopted the innovation
in spelling. It is to be hoped the incongruity of putting a
comparatively modern word before two far older, which
prevents the newer spelling ever becoming general, will
sometime be so plain as to induce a return to the more
consistent form.

This parish contained 36 families, and Edenhall 35, in
1777, the date of Burn and Nicolson's History. In Jefferson's
History, 1840, Langwathby is said to be less populous than
any parish in Leath Ward. At that date 250 was the number
of population, which is now probably doubled.

Mainly through the exertions of Miss P
the Midland Railway & S. Nich[..]
changed its modern spelling "Long-
back to [...] "Langwathby"
on their signboards & office stamp.
R. P

THE GLEANER.

"Where hast thou gleaned to-day?"—BOOK OF RUTH.

Through his lattice, unconscious, the pastor gazed,
Where now no longer the radiance blazed
Through his cottage-screen of waving pine,
Of the autumn evening's red decline.
He marked not when twilight's gloom o'erspread
The sacred page whence he late had read,
Of the old Judean harvest days,
Now given to his Fancy's backward gaze.
The leafy hum round his lonely eaves
Seems the rustling of heavy and sun-crisped sheaves,
Which with sigh of breeze and stream is blent,
And the young men's glee through the valleys sent,
'Mid their toils which the harvest maidens share,
And the daughter of Moab is gleaning there.
    Then a dearer vision before him shone,
Of a vale o'er which Alpine snow-peaks frown;
Through whose depths the waves of a blue stream
        sweep,   ·
Up whose sides the vine and the olive creep.
And reapers bend 'mid the ripened corn,
Their blythe song far on the air is borne;

And sunburnt vintagers combine
To win from the steeps their oil and wine ;
But his earliest home is fairest to view,
And those forms which the youth of his heart renew.
And the dreamer's fancy turns at last,
To think how the world is a harvest vast.
And though moveless his eye and lip remain,
Through his spirit floats this saddened strain :
  My Soul ! O, where hast thou gleaned to-day ?
And why do thy footsteps so often stray,
In the profitless fields where tares abound,
And troops of gleaners throng the ground ?
Why oft dost thou heave the silent sigh
For glades where the bowers of memory lie
By thy native streamlet's winding side,
In the pleasant sound of its rippling tide.
Where, with friends, and song, amid early flowers,
Too quickly past o'er thy spring-tide hours;
And where ne'er o'ertaken time was spent,
When first to Life's harvest a gleaner sent ?
For no sere leaf warned thy loitering feet,
'Neath the rose-arch where summer and autumn
      meet :
The forest rejoiced in its deepening green
Though white for the sickle some fields were seen.
And in orchards bent with sunburnt fruit,
The song-birds of summer were not yet mute ;
Nor fell by the stream the hoar night-dews,
Which paint on the landscape its varying hues,

Proclaiming the autumn's deepening prime,
Though 'twas barley-harvest's early time.
  That season is past, with its offered boon ;
Now is wheat-harvest's more precious noon.
More early afield comes the reaper band ;
'Tis the harvest hum pervades the land.
Ne'er so rich were the fields with green and gold ;
What azure and crimson the hills enfold !
And this brightness thou lovest, o'er nature cast,
May be summer's farewell—the last—the last !
Oh ! spend not, trifling, the precious hours,
Nor as children are wont, in gathering flowers ;
Nor faint 'neath the noontide's breezeless glare,
Nor murmur though few in thy toils may share.
For the time wears on, and at autumn's eve,
Thy spirit forlorn, shall bootless grieve—
Though the harvest-moon be full and bright—
For the wasted hours of purer light :
And, woe ! when summer is past and done,
If grace and wisdom have not been won !
  Tarry not now to bewail the past—
Why o'er thy future its shadow cast ?
Harvest is plenteous, and earth is free,
And its choicest fields may be gleaned by thee.
Onward ! afar ! by the tedious way,
Where straggling, anxious gleaners stray,
To the sun-bright slopes, to the glorious fields,
Whose soil the rich gold of garners yields ;
And gather the ears of wisdom's wheat,
Though the stubble-cares may pierce thy feet ;

Where the glorious reapers of old have trod,
The men who long since went home to God :
For the scattered wealth by their labours sown,
Hath now to a priceless harvest grown.
Look to the fields where the mighty dead,
The sweat from their laurelled brows have shed,—
To the plains of bright and immortal thought,
Whence the treasures of many a heart were brought;
Nor shrink from the steeps where, on trellised vines,
Autumn's deep day-long fervour shines.
The same pure streams from their clefts still break,
Whence the mighty of old their thirst would slake ;
And the lofty songs of their deathless age,
Shall yet thy humbler toil assuage,
As thou makest the leaf-lost wealth thine own,
Of the gleaning grapes, when the vintage is done.
  And when summer is o'er, and the joyous shout
Of Harvest-home o'er the hills rings out ;
While with sunset's soft expiring light,
Yon far-receding hills are bright,
Lift up thy voice with the sunburnt throng ;
Join in their thankful shout and song,
And cheerful, though weary, take up thy load—
The moon shall illumine thy homeward road,
And slumber such chains shall o'er thee throw,
As childhood and labour alone may know.
Then let wintry days of gloom come on,
When flowers are few, and fruit may be none ;
The treasure by faithful labour stored,
In age shall furnish the spirit's board,
And at earth's last harvest thy Lord may say,
Servant ! well hast thou gleaned to-day !

BROUGH HILL BEFORE RAILROADS.

Amid the dark Westmerian hills,
Where Eden drinks her firstling rills—
The classic stream, whose graceful course
Uter Pendragon's bootless force
Was long addressed, traditions say,
To turn it from its winding way—
There is an upland, wild and bare,
On which is held an ancient fair,
Where, on St. Michael's eve and day,
When peevish grows the year, and gray,
Chapmen from all the counties round,
With wares of every sort are found ;
Of hard, or soft, or large, or small,
Displayed on many a tempting stall.
And country produce, stock and store,
Firkins and cheeses by the score,
With implements of every trade ;
And simplest garments, knit or made
In the world's nooks, where fashions ne'er
Till ten years after date appear.
Many a device of wood or horn,
The travelled wight would hold in scorn.

Rushes, well dipped in fat, for light,
To spare the price of candles " white " ;
Which only lend their costly aid,
On nights of feasting or parade,
By many a happy dalesman's hearth,
Guiltless alike of waste or dearth.
But brighter things are gleaming here,
Genevan gauds, and Berlin ware ;
Arabian scents, furs from the North,
Gems of bright gleam, but little worth ;
All the cheap trader can devise
To catch the rustic maidens' eyes.
For here is seen, in garb of pride,
The flower of all the country-side.
Lo ! ark-like caravans that boast,
Creatures from every clime and coast ;
From tropic heat and polar snows,—
Which now these narrow bounds enclose.
And here, in bondage may be seen
The roamers of our fell-sides green :
Pens of sore-soiled and trembling sheep,
And cattle tether'd on the steep,
By mud, and by the moving crowd,
Which never leaves for one a road.
Horses, in strings or droves are there,
More mettled blood their owners bear.
Ponies that on wide moors had strayed,
Of every size, and shape, and shade ;
Which ne'er have felt the rein or bit,
Now tired, amazed, perforce submit ;

Though long they rear, and kick, and snort,-
Causing the crowd no little sport.
And antics—Punch and many a show,
Whose trumpeter walks to and fro ;
And, with untiring zeal and din,
Invites admiring gazers in.
And liquor tents, where cheer and glass,
With every match and bargain, pass ;
Where drouthy swains sit snug and warm,
While roars without the brawl or storm.
Sunburnt Bavarians shout their brooms,
'Twixt sighs for their far southern homes ;
Like those dark-eyed Italian boys,
Whose music swells the wondrous noise,
With fiddle, bagpipe, shout, laugh, neigh,
Bleat, grunt, crow, cackle, hiss, and bray—
These rue the day, for gain they sought,
So late, this upland wild remote.
For oft upon St. Michael's day,
The elements seem in a fray.
But vainly storm or driving hail
The hardy northern wights assail ;
The rain may pour, or frost may pinch,
They stir not from their post an inch.
Jobbers and sharpers carp and jangle ;
And jolly 'statesmen greet, or wrangle,
And haply, to as wise conclusion,
As in St. Stephen's great confusion.
And farmers *look* more wise by far,
Than merely mortals ever are ;

By coats and plaids.swelled out in size,
And 'kerchief muffled to their eyes.
Here one, well wrapped, holds loudly forth,
On what *this* beast, and *that* is worth ;
Whipping his brown topped-boots—the pair
Time out of mind, seen at the fair—
While at his heart, through all his coats,
His pocket-book the sharper notes ;
And in some swaying crowd, and dense,
Subtracts it from his consequence :
For pickpockets are met from far,
As ravens on the field of war.
While drenching rains, and winds so shrill
Oft sweep the high unsheltered hill,
That now, all sorts of storm together,
Is curtly called Brough-Hillish weather.
    No spot indeed, in all the land,
Such frequent mention may command,
As this, the Northmen's mart of old,
Where yearly higgled, bought, and sold,
Their sires ; who from each far deep dale,
By rugged fell-side roads would scale,
When crops were housed, and minds at rest,
With long-anticipated zest,
T' enjoy, as still both great and small,
Enjoy this rural carnival,—
The grand excitement of their life,
Where news and enterprise were rife ;
Where flashed on many a dalesman raw,
All of the world he ever saw.

No mention made of tide or time,
This name with them stands out sublime,
For Autumn's shortening drizzly days,
For leafless trees, and miry ways.
You'd think the spot was classic ground
Whose name on all men's lips is found.
Farmers and traders, housewives—all
Date from this famous carnival ;
And sportsmen, if you ask, reply,
That first the woodcock—rare and shy,—
In northern plashes dips his bill,
" The first full-moon after Brough Hill."
And rushes cut 'neath that same light,
The housewife knows, will burn most bright ;
And, ask the date of bond or bill,
'Tis often,—just about Brough Hill.
All change that Autumn brought, or brings,
The flight of birds, or fall of kings,
Is linked,—though great or small th' event,
With this, to them, more prominent.
Not Stratford, nay—not Runnymede—
No scene of deathless birth or deed,
Whose name may History's pages fill,
Enjoys such fame as bleak Brough Hill.
And did they name some fight of yore,
As Hastings, or as Agincourt,
Which happened while the sere leaves lay,
Though many a hundred miles away,
The Northern rustics' utterance still,
Would have it—" just about Brough Hill."

Should they bethink them,—'twas this day,
On which the Conqueror sailed away,
'Gainst England, in his power and state,
St. Michael to propitiate—-
(The Normans' ancient patron-Saint,)
By prayers, and by observance quaint,—
They'd say, and think no jest or ill,
The Conqueror sailed about Brough Hill.
   But, should a stranger, spirit-stirred,
By that which he might *think* he heard,
Of treasure lost, of empire won,—
Deeds of high faith and valour done,
Which ancient prophecies fulfil—
All *at* this very same Brough Hill.
Where births, deaths, marriages seem rife,
Bad accidents, and loss of life ;
Where household stuff, and clothes were bought,
Pockets were picked, and fevers caught—
The scene of fun, and fraud, and vice ;
The mart of various merchandise,—
And seek the spot, save where the fair
Makes life, and stir, and traffic there,
He well might doubt this height so bleak,
Could be the spot he came to seek ;—
The storied, trophied, classic hill,
Which fancy furnishes at will ;
And like the traveller old, enquire,
" If this could be the Northern Tyre ?"

"AND THIS ALSO SHALL PASS AWAY."

"There is an oriental tale of a Sultan who consulted
Solomon on the proper inscription for a signet ring, requiring
that the maxim which it conveyed should be at once proper
for moderating the presumption of prosperity, and tempering
the pressure of adversity. The apophthegm supplied by the
Jewish sage, was I think admirably adapted for both pur-
poses, being comprised in the words—And this also shall
pass away."—*Letter of Sir W. Scott. Lockhart's Life.*

O, warning meet for triumph's hour !
   When to the conqueror's feet are brought
The trophies of his fearful power,
   Of glorious deeds his arm had wrought.
But dim his eye and sad his soul
   As swells the Pæan shout on high ;
Remorse and pity o'er him stole,—
   The warning signet met his eye.
The pageant fades like morning's breath,
   His towering pride hath lost its stay :
In visions of reverse and death,
   He sees that this shall pass away.

The captive on whose brightening chain
   Many a sad summer's light hath shone,
Starts, weeps,—as the spring-beams again
   Find him still captive and alone.

But yet—within his breast revives
  Of hope deferred the expiring ray.
His heart is free, his courage lives—
  This yet, on earth may pass away.
At least, the tyrant's boon of breath,
  Consum'd in sighs that speak his sway,
The anguish of this living death,—
  He knows that these shall pass away.

When day departs, and footsteps cease
  Around the sick man's lonely bed ;
And midnight stillness brings not peace,
  Nor slumbers, to his feverish head.
Yet bears he on.   Still prayers ascend
  Of faith, amid the mortal strife ;
And drops of Heaven's own balm descend
  O'er failing heart, and brain, and life.
He knows the bleeding ties which strain
  Th' aspiring spirit down to clay—
The gloom—the bitterness—the pain
  Of even Death shall pass away.

Through hours which healthful sleep should claim,
  The student toils with painful care ;
In hectic haste to climb to Fame,
  And pluck the wreath he ne'er shall wear.
For Fame's, nor Wisdom's beams renew
  Youth's radiant bloom, and green delight ;
And sad Affection's tears bedew
  In vain, its unreviving blight.

He dreamed in future days, to give
   Some boon to men—some truth to say;
To teach the dead in sin, to live—
   And woke—but life had passed away.

The warning speaks in accents low,
   But deep, to all of human clay;
The doom of joy—the knell of woe,
   For both alike shall pass away.
On all of Life is written—Death;
   A shade of change is on each leaf;
Sorrow like vapour vanisheth,
   And joy, alas! is yet more brief.
Only the Christian's hope and faith
   Is fixed on one pure, steadfast ray,
Which lights the gloomy vale of Death
   When Earth and Time have passed away.

SOLON.

A HISTORICAL SKETCH.

A tumult rose in Athens old,
    Amid the market's space ;
A great and gathering crowd behold
    With eager, upraised face ;
One in a sick man's garb arrayed,
    And cap, who stood on high,
Whose tones of power the clouds invade,
    While fiery gleamed his eye ;
And all were mute, save he alone,
The bard who stood on the heralds' stone.

'Twas a son of Codrus' race who dared
    A strain unheard to sing ;
And the pitying people knew and spared
    The blood of their martyr-king.
Nor voice was raised to check his song,
    Nor hand a brand to draw,
On him who 'mid the city's throng,
    Outraged the dastard law ;
Which doomed his death who counselled this,
War for lost, severed Salamis.

'Twas Solon, who indignant, sheathed
　　Till now, his patriot aim ;
And o'er Megærian triumphs, wreathed
　　With Athens' sunken name,
Had brooded,—madman-like the while,—
　　Lest to his lips should swell
His theme of thought, his native isle
　　Which his sires had loved so well.
And his soul fulfilled its task in this—
Singing a song of Salamis.

And soon in the fervid atmosphere
　　Of his patriot energy
Their souls grew warm, their eyes saw clear
　　For Athens, Victory ;
As he bade them with a Prophet's might,
　　To break their spirits' chain,
And win the isle that shone so bright
　　In the blue Saronic main ;
Or die,—as their fathers died, for this
Their isle of refuge, Salamis.

In many a breast Resolve grew strong
　　That had not died, but slept ;
And Valour's tongue was loosed, that long
　　Silence perforce had kept.
The patriot Sage's artifice
Won back for Athens Salamis.

Nor, in our boasted times, in sooth,
    Are men and things so changed;
Or hearts less hardly won to Truth
    That Error hath estranged.
Teachers more high, in faith more blest,
    With him may still believe—
" Those laws and lessons still are best
    Which men can best receive."
And deign to conquer prejudice,
Like him the Sage of Salamis.

Oft, to stern Blame impervious,
    Men Error closer hold,
As, spite the blasts of Æolus,
    His cloak the wight of old ;
Who, when the sun shone, still and warm,
    Cast its dark folds aside ;
So softer influences disarm
    Perversity and Pride.
As once the Lawgiver and Sage,
Roused with a song his torpid age.

EASTER DAY IN COUNTRY CHURCHES
IN CUMBERLAND. 1848.

The Lord hath risen to-day!
Shall many a glad heart say;
And in these northern valleys deep and lone,
Beauty is disentombed;
Nature, which seemed benumbed,
From the Spring's sepulchre hath rolled away the
stone.

In village churches gray,
In chapels far away,
Under some verdant hill or sheltering rock;
Some Sabbath gathering place,
For wide thin peopled space,
Weekly the pastor feeds his scattered mountain flock.

The traveller scarce might note
The humble pile remote,
Save for the field-paths from its gate diverging;
One spans the fell's bleak brow,
One in the vale below
Lost, till on some bright hamlet-green emerging.

In windows barred and low,
No blazoned emblems show,
No tracery is wrought about the lowly eaves ;
Nor round these pillars climb
Carved wreaths, save those of time,
But sunshine falls unstained through ever-wavering
leaves.

No storied 'scutcheons wave
O'er knight's or noble's grave—
Such never dwelt or slept in this green dell ;
Nor from the Holy Wars,
Came one with glorious scars
To give to these low walls a boastful tale to tell.

But where their fathers prayed—
Where their own dead are laid—
Comes many a Sabbath group by field and shady lanes ;
Parents, with pious thought,
Where they of old were brought,
Bring children to be taught within these lowly fanes.

And, as the childish band
In solemn order stand,
Before the holy man in his high robes and place,
Who catechising each,
Hears in his shrill small speech,
And accents quaint, each child his creed and duties
trace.

Seems it not very meet,
In pastoral valleys sweet,
At intervals 'twixt prayer and praise and psalms,
That thus should be obeyed
His high behest, Who said
Of old, to His apostles, "Feed my lambs"?

Perchance they little know,—
The motley lisping row,—
Of all the mighty depth and import of their words;
But such is oft, me seems,
The sowing by all streams
Of seed whose fruit shall be in after years, the Lord's.

Scarce shall it be forgot,
That in this hallowed spot,
Such strength for life or death, was to their weakness
    given;
While men in sins grown grey,
Hearing their children pray,
Have felt that yet one link remained 'twixt them
    and Heaven.

I have often heard the children say their
Catechism to the Vicar, standing in a row
in the aisle before the reading desk.
There was no Pulpit in the place for
it. But I do not remember if it
were Castle Carrock   P. P.

THE PETRIFIED FOREST,

NEAR GRAND CAIRO.

What rings beneath our horses' tread,
　Like iron in this desert vale,
With sinking sand and sea-shells spread—
　Where round us dismal hues prevail?

A forest fallen—a maze of stone—
　Which scarce th' Egyptian ass may thread.
Rigid, and desolate, and prone,—
　Dead—darkly, and forever dead.

When forests leave our hills and plains,
　Their rooted still-life seems to change,
For one which human art ordains,—
　A lower life—with wider range.

In form of stately ships, the oak
　May cruise and compass oft the world;
Its top, where spring-birds warbling woke,
　May bear the British flag unfurled.

ᴛhe rafters that our roofs uphold,
  Those doors that keep the storm at bay,
The staff that props us, weak and old ;
  The coffin that protects our clay,

These, man's allies—seem not dead things :
  But in this sterile vale, and lone,
Ghastly as mummies of their kings,
  Forever lie these trunks of stone.

The fibres still, the roots we trace,
  The bark—and where 'tis broke apart,
Discern how, in its sylvan days,
  The worm assailed the giant's heart.

O ! change how dismal here, since bowed
  Those rigid boughs, with every breeze
Which, passing woke, and swept abroad,
  The varied voice of living trees.

Each tree gave forth its own sweet tone ;
  Each, haply, bore some genial bird,
Whose plumage from our world is gone,
  Whose song may never more be heard.

No sound of axe, no lightning's scath,
  No slow decay those trunks have known ;
Crept through their veins insidious Death,
  And turned their very worm to stone.

In all the landscape now no palm
 Waves, cooling the hot sultry air ;
No bright bird seeks the forest's calm,
 To build, or rest, or warble there.

No cedar shades the scorching beams,
 Nor date tree bends with luscious fruit ;
The smitten vale forsaken seems,
 And the hot breezes faint and mute.

Ruins mysterious ! as the pile
 Round which Doubt's mists are ever curled ;
Are ye of Egypt's ancient growth,
 Or wrecks of some dim deluged world ?

No power unbinds your stony chains ;
 No second life from man's decrees,
No pile consumes your dark remains ;
 Ye hopeless sylvan Sadducees !

O, dismal types ! Thank God our faith
 Saves Christians from such sleep forlorn ;
Though dark, though sudden, sad our death,
 We waken to a brighter morn.

NOTE.

"Nice observers of Nature have remarked on the variety of tones yielded by trees when played on by the wind. Mrs. Hemans once asked Sir Walter Scott, if he had noticed that every tree gives out its peculiar sound, 'Yes,' said he, 'I have, and I think something might be done by the union of poetry and music to imitate their voices, giving a different measure to the oak, the pine, the willow.' What a contrast to a living forest, moving and vocable in every breeze, is that remarkable spectacle—the petrified Forest near Grand Cairo! The traveller having passed the tombs of the Caliphs just beyond the City gates, proceeds southward across the Desert to Suez," &c.—*Tait's Magazine, October,* 1846.

THE PASS OF THE ICEBERGS.

SUGGESTED BY THE ACCOUNT OF THE UNITED
STATES EXPLORING EXPEDITION, 1838-42.

O ! little the sailor, though veteran he be,
   Knows of perils or storms of the ocean,
Whose course has been over waves liquid and free,
   Though with winds in the fiercest commotion ;
If he hath not been tossed on the dark winter sea,
Where more cruel than earth-rocks the ice-billows be.

Our ship her brave course through the far Polar deep
   Was swiftly, but heedfully cleaving ;
That her frost-bitten crew her prompt mastery might
     keep,
   For the ice-rocks were clashing and heaving ;
With the surges' wild swell, or the snow-driving gale—
Perils dire as the Argo's of old Grecian tale.

How beauteous and pure in our boyhood we deemed
　　The snow-wreath that crowned our own Highland;
And the snow, through our Yule-lighted casement
　　　　had seemed
　　Like a holiday garb of the island;
But here, 'twas a shroud, ghastly, hateful as white,
To veil which we blest e'en the perilous night.

On our food, was the snow, on our sails, on our bed;
　　The ice mountains seemed sepulchres whited,
Of long perished ships,—snow encumbered our tread,
　　And the low-sailing clouds were snow-freighted;
And for weeks not a leaf, not a bird had been seen;
All was whiteness abhorred, save the sea's sullen
　　　　green.

And all canvass was crowded, to windward to keep
　　From the rocks where the surf was heard roaring;—
Uncharted, unseen—the still growth of the deep;—
　　And we felt, with the blinding snow pouring,
How near to a monster, blind, ruthless, and vast,
When, aback, by the eddy, our try-sails were cast.

Icebergs passed, like bears foiled, hoarsely growled
　　　　on the stern,
　　By their shocks the ship's timbers were bending;
Yet, less certain seemed death in advance than return,
　　Though the low sun scarce twilight was lending:
But a gust helped the horror-struck helm's-man to spy
An ice-wall which towered on each side to the sky.

Then burst forth that dread, dream-haunting shout—
    " Ice ahead ! "
By—"And close on the weather-bow !" followed;
"On the lee-boom!—abeam!" it was instantly said—
And the tempest more fearfully bellowed :
Then Hope seemed to have plunged 'neath the dark
    swirling wave,
And the thick snow was shed as the dust o'er a grave.

And the vessel rushed on with her heart-stagnant
    crew,—
Ever dauntless and true to their duty in danger,—
Skill was naught—nor their old bootless bravery
    now ;
But an impulse of prayer—to some hearts long a
    stranger—
With the home-pang of dying afar, like a flash,
Shot through hearts of the death-bolt awaiting the
    crash.

Eyes unconsciously glared on the horrible rift,
    Whose jaws to escape, but a maniac had striven :
To her doom goes the ship,—with the impetus swift
    Which her masters—aeriel and human—have
        given !
O, suspense ! the next agony life has to death !—
Save that man may survive—and once more we
    drew breath.

Lo ! as passed through the Red Sea the Israelites
  old,
  As the dove-guided Argo 'twixt floating rocks
  steered,
Straight and swift as the flashing aurora—behold—
  The death-gorge, all scathless the gallant ship
  cleared !
And grey tars view with thankful, yet doubtful amaze,
The strait none had dared in his boldest of days.

To be storm-tossed was joy—conscious life in the
  shocks—
  E'en to bend through the white haze our snow-
  troubled vision ;
Or list the wild whistling 'twixt huge wandering rocks,
  Which the fierce sea may lash into awful collision.
Chart nor beacon shall mark them, nor eye see again;
Their stern life is unbound in the soft southern main.

And oft, like a man who at midnight must trust
  His life to some dark guide he may not believe,
But walks with a hand raised to guard his false
  thrust—
  To an iceberg the lone ship is anchored at eve ;
And watchfully drifts in its wide-sweeping wake,
Till dim morn on the long fearful darkness shall
  break.

And perils unknown—dismal deaths none can tell—
  Ships like ancient live victims forever immured,
By the waves' stony walls—and, hark ! to their yell,
  Who ere death, horror, hunger, and madness
    endured !
God Almighty ! the lost and the wanderer to keep,
Guide the course of the brave on the far Polar deep !

ON AN ANCIENT GRAVE,

DISCOVERED ON LANGWATHBY MOOR, FEB.—1850.

A Grave! Where the sower would scatter his seed,
 In this nook of the vale, by the lone moorland
  rill ;—
'Neath the stone that no longer the plough may
  impede,
 Though for undisturbed ages it crowned the green
  hill.

But what people, or age, may this dust have
  bequeathed
 To the lone valley's keeping, no record hath
  traced ;
What rites have been practised, what prayers have
  been breathed,
 When this rude grave of Honour was made in the
  Waste.

For of honour it tells.—As this mound the deep
    vale,
So thy fame, nameless dust ! once thy brethren's
    surpassed,—
And the urn in thy sepulchre, uncouth and frail,
    Speaks of friends, and their cares for thy soul as it
    passed.

And men tell us—"Some Chief of the Britons lies
    here ";
Men who vast tomes of history, haply have
    scanned,
But who see not the signs in our pathway so clear—
    The Runes that are writ on this people and land.

When the names of our hamlets and hills meet my
    ear,
Or our rude Northern tongue, unenfeebled by time;
When the voice of our fathers' stern Fiend's-fell
    I hear,
    Like a Skald's who is chanting a requiem sublime;

Then this spot conjures up some wild tale of the
    North,—
For a spell lures me back, as to kindred remains;
And in fancy I see o'er the hill-tops break forth,
    A cloud of the restless, all-conquering Danes.

Herds again stray at will through this vale, waste
    and bleak,
And from huts on the hill waving smoke-wreaths
    ascend ;
While the strong man's defiance, the wail of the weak,
    Seem, with clang of rude arms, and fast trampling
    to blend.

Red fires, through the darkness mark many a far
    height ;
But the strength of the valleys is gathered in vain :
How fierce is the shock of the merciless fight !
    How thick at its close lie the maimed and the
    slain !

And again floats the Raven of Denmark on high,
    By the brook ;—yet the victors in sadness appear,—
Ah ! they raise their stern leader ! it is but to die,
    And the voice of the dying is borne to my ear.

"Let me lie in this vale, which my prowess hath
    won,
    As is meet for a Jarl, and a warrior to lie !
'Neath a grave-mound befitting my father's renown ;
    He who went on the sea in his fire-ship to die !

" But alone—all alone—not my weapons or steed,
   Shall be laid in the breast of this alien land ;
Those faithful and tried ones, my son, thou wilt need,
   When the Thane shall have strengthened his
     fugitive band.

" And I, who am favoured by Alfaders' grace—
   A warrior chosen in battle to die,
Valhalla's bright sons shall my weapons replace—
   Farewell ! for their splendour now dazzles my
     eye ! "

It is done.   And while this lowly grave keeps its
   trust,
   Gods and temples have perished, and Empires
     declined ;
On the red creed of Odin lie ages of rust ;
   And the Gospel of Peace is the bond of mankind.

Yet once more,—I could dream 'twas this brave son
   who cast
   At the feet of stern Cross-fell his spoils of the main;
And made those green slopes,—spite the Thane and
   the blast—
   The prize, and thenceforward, the home of the
     Dane.

The name of one hamlet bears record alone
  Of lost triumphs, which Fancy would image—in
    vain ;
His deeds are forgotten, his grave is unkown,
  But tradition still points where dwelt Melmor the
    Dane.

NOTE.

The grave was certainly British, as far as the urn and manner
of burial could prove it so.   This imaginary view of the grave
and its occupant has no other ground than, that the locality,
and the names around, were favourable to a dream of what
might have been.

The writer's consciousness of the absence of weapons, or
other usual accompaniments of a Northman's grave-mound, is
implied in the dying hero's words.

INVOCATION TO PATIENCE.

O, Patience ! Friend and Healer, stern yet kind ;
Look, where we struggle in Affliction's throe,
And lend thy soothing balm,—the soft and slow—
Yet sure, our sad and world-worn hearts to bind.

Pilgrim, and Seer, and Sage ! Born of old Time,
And Wisdom ; let us lowly at thy feet,
Oft list to thy mild utterance, replete
With teachings of thy parentage sublime.

Of old thou wert a Stoic ; and beneath
The pillared fane, unmoved, stood'st looking out;
While War's and Superstition's reckless rout
Made straight earth's paths for the old conqueror,
Death.

Nor smitten flowers, nor friends crushed in his way,
Wrung from thy iron heart one frigid sigh ;
Nor teardrop dimmed thy clear and steadfast eye,
When in its sight earth's loveliest dying lay.

But now thou art a Christian, and thy heart
Of flesh, though inly sound, hath suffered sore ;
And through thy mild eyes Nature's sorrows pour,
And oft, men see thee sitting sad, apart ;

Yet tranquil, and with often upward glance ;
Or, through steep paths of thorny duty wending,
Wrong-stricken, with pierced feet; or meekly
bending,
'Neath clouds of dark afflictive circumstance.

Or, musing by the stream, where willow boughs
Seem flowing with its waves, yet fixed abide ;
As good men seem to flow with the world's tide,
Yet their high place and purpose never lose.

Or, in Life's highway, halting oft to aid
The weak and faint, the erring to bring back
To the pure sunshine of the Christian's track ;
Tending the fallen in the wayside shade.

O, good Samaritan, and guide ! could'st teach
Our faltering feet to hold th' appointed race ;
Our shrinking souls Life's far-seen blasts to face,
Our eyes to view bright flowers we may not reach.

5

Aid us to banish far the thankless pride
  With which, like children spoilt we turn,
  And many a precious blessing spurn,
If one wild wish may not be gratified.

Make us by heart,—not lip, or ear, to learn
  How worse than bootless is our earnest will;—
  How vain man's proud and mountain-moving
    skill,
To shun the darts no mortal shield may turn.

Disciple of Faith, Hope, and Charity!
  Of each the nature and the grace partaking;
  Lend us thine arm to stay this purpose-shaking,
To reach, through storms, Heaven's bright tran-
    quillity.

Patience! what lessons beam from thy Seraphic
    face!
  'Mid creeds and schools, but One hath taught
    like thee:—
  Not of the earth thy pure benignity;—
Angelic is its sphere, its name is Heavenly Grace.

ENGLAND,

THE MEADOW LAND.

England ! Methinks thou wert The Meadow Land,
   To olden rovers of the North seas known ;
Though, round thy southward coasts the white
     cliffs stand,
  And Roman legions called thee Albion.
But to their eyes who sailed the chill seas o'er
   So oft, from darker tracts, of the high North ;
Who named that islet, Meadowland,—by Holstein
     shore,
  Wert thou not, ages long, the gem of earth ?
  Thy sward and shore, the charms, brought many
     a longing rover forth ?

Wide, with fair woods, with grassy holms and hills,
   Sunshine and showery skies, they saw thee stand;
With noble streams, the sum of gathered rills ;
  Apart-- a rich, majestic meadow land.

And when late spring to their stern clime returned;
　　When the hoar-frost died out the north-sea breeze,
And Viking hearts again for conquest burned,
　　　As Egir sunk the ice in softened seas,
　　　Thou wert the loadstar of their hopes, their
　　　　energies.

Came not rude barks, then fleets, age after age,
　　In thy spring verdure, haunting shore and creek;
With fierce fresh hordes, the welcome war to wage,
　　And force resistless dispossessed the weak?
In Cumbria's slowly changing vales, we now,—
　　As favoured flocks graze deep, in early springs,
On river-meads unbroken by the plough,
　　　Of perfect verdure—call them holms and ings,*
　　　And Fancy oft, o'er these old names, a Runic
　　　　radiance flings.

---

* *Eng*, Icelandic and Danish, a meadow. *Holm*, Ice. and
Dan., once—an island, now often the raised bank of a river.
Eng, or *Ing*, as we spell it, seems to belong to those districts
considered more decidedly Danish, and is so generally found
in conjunction with the termination *by*, that it might perhaps
serve, also, as a sort of test-word of long Danish occupation.
In many old agricultural parishes it is a field name, both in
south Cumberland and Westmorland. In Langwathby, there
is a parcel of joint proprietorship named *open Ings*—besides
private Ings—not adjoining a river. In Yorkshire the word
is well known in the same Danish sense, and there are large
tracts so named—some of 100 acres. From the source of the
Eden to some miles below Penrith, *Ing* is found in the names
of many meadowy farms, in both counties—as Little Ing,
Load Ing, Lady Ing, Hard Ing, Broad Ing, West Ing, Pye
Ing, Lambeck Ing, etc.; all which are invariably, properly
accented in speaking, but sometimes sadly confused in writing,
by joining the two words.

O, verdurous Isle! If thus in old times known,
Favoured by gleam and shower, fanned by each
    breeze,
That grassy wealth yet strangers call thine own,
Which none hath found in other lands or seas.
And needless thus, to that small Anglen horde
'T were, greater tribes should bow, to name the
    strand;
Saxon, Dane, Northmen, Angles,—in accord,
Might sheath their strife 'neath that old, happy
    word:
Call themselves, proud as we—still a mixt band,—
Thenceforward, English—Children of the Meadow
    Land.

1858.

NOTE.

In Marryatt's *Jutland and the Danish Isles*, he says: "The frequent mention of England's Holm, England's this, and England's that, at first puzzled me. The word *Eng*, signifies meadow, and *England* is merely common parlance for meadow-land."

English may often, in Denmark, refer to the meadowy district of Holstein.

Historians say the record does not clearly show why the smaller tribe of invaders should have given name to this country, and various reasons are given for the circumstance.

"At least as early as the 10th century the Saxons who had formed settlements in England, called the language Englisc, and the country Englaland. King Alfred also, though of

West Saxon origin, uses these appellations; and abroad in the Scandinavian countries and in Iceland, the country was in the 10th century called England, and the nation Englar, or Enzkir menn.   The monks of that age too, in writing Latin, called the nation Angli, which obviously points to the Angles.   It may be rather difficult now to account for this circumstance in a satisfactory manner; for the total emigration of the Angles seems not to afford any sufficient reason for these appellations of English and England;—since it is certain that they were in numerical respect, a smaller tribe than the Saxons, and that not they, but the Saxons were the leaders, as well during the invasion as after settling in the country. Perhaps it is a more admissible reason that as the East Angles occupied that part of the British coast on which Danes and Norwegians most frequently landed, the appellation English, was first promiscuously applied by them to all the Teutonic tribes that had settled in the country, and afterwards adopted by the natives themselves ; the more readily since it had the advantage of distinguishing them from their Saxon brethren on the continent."—*Int. to Repp's Danish Dictionary.*

THE WOMAN OF MIND.

A PARODY.*

(Written for Edenhall Penny Readings, 1867.)

My wife, too, 's a woman of mind ;
   Though on no phrenological tests,—
On proofs practical, moral, domestic—
   Her mental certificate rests.
Though I don't like a flourish of trumpets,
   Nor think angels e'er dwell with mankind,
We may set on the right horse the saddle,
   And do justice to women of mind.

Howe'er lofty in gifts or attainment,
   As ladies in plenty you 'll find ;
If good sense and plain duty 's neglected,
   I call it perversion of mind.
If too clever to care for appearance,
   If for home-wear too proud or refined,
If she oftener *says* "good things" than *does* them,
   A fig for such woman of mind.

* On a piece which was often heard at Penny Readings,
beginning, "My wife is a woman of mind."

My wife 's not a bit like my neighbour's,—
    Has no blue-stocking haughty pretence;
When she tells me "*a bit of her mind,*"
    'Tis with wonderful tact and good sense.
Neither proud of her bumps nor her learning,
    She is happily able to find
Distinction and pride in her duties,
    Enough for her well-balanced mind.

She can do any stitch,—for adorning—
    Repairing—of household or clothes;—
I never find shirts without buttons,
    Nor stockings with holes at the toes.
She scorns not the homely and useful,
    Says all labour by love is refined;
Calls the darning of stockings, a poem,
    To a good wife and woman of mind.

She can make, when she likes, themes and verses,
    But oftener makes puddings and tarts;
Knows how acids and alkalies mingle,
    And such useful and chemical arts.
And she knows, too, a good man's affection
    Disregard or neglect may unbind;
That *an Englishman holds by his dinner,*—
    And she acts—like a woman of mind.

I'm not deafened by squalling of children,
    Love and firmness good order maintain;
And my wife has a care for the units,—
    As the millions—of money or men.

And while first for her nearest and dearest,
  Unselfish, and thoughtful, and kind ;
For the good of the wide human family,
  Is striving the woman of mind.

Her quick eye prevents peculations,
  No servant could sell from *our* store ;
And in prices and quantities, knowing,
  My wife keeps the wolf from the door.
For she knows that the housekeeping 's heavy,
  And that care helps the money to find ;
That, though dross, it buys credit and comfort,
  In the hands of a woman of mind.

Our furniture 's bright as a mirror,
  The servants are prompt and polite,
'Gainst all pests, parasitic or pendant,
  Or flying or crawling, unite
Fresh air and pure water in plenty ;
  And, 'neath her good guidance combined,
Health, cleanliness, good-taste,—distinguish
  The home of my woman of mind.

When of authors we chat, never jealous,
  (Oft to both the same favourites are dear)—
If I write—I've a lively home-critic ;
  If I sing—I've a sweet echo near.
And while reading—from Milton to Bulwer,
  Or what author I choose, I'm not blind
To the pleased and discerning reflection,
  On the face of my woman of mind.

And on Sundays,—at church with her children,
   Whom she leads in the time-honoured way,—
No worshipper there is so humble,
   Though she knows much the parson will say.
None so well knows how high aspiration
   Must ever leave practice behind;
And that there rich and poor are all equal,—
   As the Christian, and woman of mind.

TO PENRITH BEACON.

Ho ! Warder of the breezy steep,
  Again unto the world awaking !
After thy forty years of sleep
  Another day is breaking.
Long years of peace had blessed the land,
  Ere woods their curtain round thee drew ;*
And ne'er hath come a hostile band,
  This hundred years for thee to view.

Like older, prouder fanes, art thou—
  Whose aim is lost, whose fires are cold,—
Alien from all around thee now,
  A voucher for the tales of old.
But, when these vales were scantly tilled—
  Those hills were wildly bare and bleak,
Oft to thy lonely height there thrilled
  The trampling rush—the shout—the shriek.

---

* The Spire of the Beacon has again been given to view,
by the order of Lord Lonsdale for the cutting down the trees
immediately round it, since which the two first verses were
altered.

As blazed thy far o'erseeing spire,
　A pillar of disastrous light ;
And distant hills replied, with fire
　To that dread signal of the night.
Dismay the country-side o'erspread,
　None knowing where the bolt should fall ;
The ravaged hearth, and lawless raid
　Anticipation dealt to all.

Proud Sentinel ! Look down and see—
　If thee alone, no joy it yields—
How Cultivation's 'broidery
　Now wraps those barren skirmish fields !
Calm fanes of prayer—sweet homes, behold—
　Where panted once scared Solitude !
And pasturing herds, where outlaws bold
　Hunted the wild deer of the wood.

Where once a monarch—on a day,
　Long, long ere rose thy spire to view,—
Sent from his quiver shafts,—they say,
　Two sylvan hecatombs that slew.*
And where in earlier ages gone,
　Successive hordes invading came,
See peaceful men, from sire to son,
　The same few fertile acres claim.

---

* "So full of deer was the ancient forest of Inglewood,
that Edward the first, when returning victorious from Scotland, is said to have killed 200 bucks in a few days."

Our fathers in their day fulfilled
   Their part, a wild and stormy lot.
And, grudge not that their sons now tread
   A path where foes and fame are not.
And see'st thou not, as sunlight fills
   The vales, o'er woods thou peerest forth,
Still, gatherings 'mid the Cumbrian hills,
   And rural Risings in the North?

What! scorn'st thou the heroic name,
   To lowly men and deeds applied,
Of that old strife,—of fearful fame—
   'Twixt regal power, and lordly pride?*
Yet wherefore? are not sword and brand
   With which our fathers fought of yore
To ploughshares turned, to till the land—
   Waste and debateable no more?

On thoughts, while that old phrase is breathed
   This later use no shame shall cast;
For kings and bards with flowers have wreathed
   The Grecian plough in ages past.

---

* The Rising in the North.
"After the comparatively unimportant insurrection which became so celebrated through the fine heroic ballad, *The Rising in the North*, the Duke of Sussex and Sir George Bowes put to death numbers by martial law. One of them boasted that, for 60 miles in length, and 40 in breadth, there was hardly a town or village in which he had not executed some of the inhabitants."—*Percy's Reliques.*

The glory of that fearful day
  Whose name so sacred thou would'st hold,
Cheered not that night of blood and woe,
  Of which old chroniclers have told.

Nor broke the 'vengeful shower, that swift
  On threescore ravaged miles did fall;
And Death and Desolation left
  In town and hamlet, bower and hall.
This morn—which Winter doth not claim—
  Nor Spring's ethereal mildness own,—
Grey changeling from the flowery time
  Which songs from olden bards hath won,—

Hath yet a charm e'en thou might'st feel,
  Stone heart! as Fame or Glory cold!
The warmth which kindly deeds exhale
  Might melt thy frozen pride of old.
To till their neighbour's land, three-score
  Of goodly teams this morning came;
A band as prompt as when of yore
  Steep called to steep with tongue of flame.

Now many a ploughshare glances bright,
  And many a voice is raised in glee;
And gazers,—patriots—hail the sight,
  The Rising of the stout and free.
The freeman's boon, on peaceful field,
  Unlike the service of the sword,
When men their day, or life must yield,
  At mandate of some tyrant lord.

And see ! the foreign raid to bar,
Starts to its feet a stalwart band ;
From folds among the hills afar,
From all the cities of the land.
Hoping for peace—for war prepared—
Up rise the unaggressive hosts ;
'Gainst their protest, no foe hath dared ;—
Their spirit fitly guards our coasts.

And, round one well-stored board will soon
Be met,—scarce tired,—that kindly throng :
Who gave by day his labour-boon,
At evening gives his jovial song.
For arts that cheer,—enrich the earth,—
Long may we friendly Risings see !
But never more our beauteous North,
Wasted,—as oft 't was seen by thee !

NOTE.

It is pleasant to be told that the steam plough can never, in this district, entirely supersede the older plough, with its manifold associations and advantages ; and that from circumstances of country and climate, the good custom of ploughing days is in no danger of being lost, in new ways. It is one of the advantages of a mixture of large and small properties and farms, that a new tenant, entering on his farm, whether large or small, can have the assistance of so many of his agricultural neighbours—for asking—on an appointed day, to prepare his ground at once, for the seed. The numbers are sometimes larger than those mentioned above ; which implies that the farm is a large one, and that some must have travelled several miles to reach the place. Thirty, I am told, is a more usual number of *draughts*—the local word for *team*—as there are more smaller, than large farms. There is often honourable competition on these public occasions, which can make the best work. Refreshments are ample, spirits high, and at the end of the day, an excellent dinner, with proper accompaniments ; and social enjoyment and song. These are called *boon days* with more justice than the old exactions of feudal times—and are quite voluntary.

FRIENDS.

What are our friends? and what are we, their benefits
    to scan ?
Ere Reason dawned or Memory woke, their loving
    care began,
And shall survive our consciousness ; for in Life's
    uncertain round,—
Our faith is firm—good friends and true, shall unto
    Death be found.
What cause for grateful thought is ours—how little
    good were left,
If all we've gained from wiser heads, and higher
    hearts were reft.
From the cradle to the bier their influence extends,
O ! poorest on the earth, though crowned—the
    destitute of friends !

Instruction, habits, characters—what are they but
    the hues
Reflected from the friends we love, whose choice
    we ever choose ?
Well-remembered fire-side counsel, in tones of
    friends of old,
A power like words of oracles, in after years must
    hold ;

And if 'neath the world's unkindness, or strangers'
    wrongs we smart,
The thought is balm—there is a friend who better
    knows my heart!
True friends! whose cheer, in Sorrow's depth, or
    Fortune's dark despite,
To us, like constant brooks, would give their songs
    throughout the night.

Fond Hope and wistful Memory each their influence
    partake;
All our visions of the future are brighter for their
    sake;
And past—how large the share of friends! though
    some are dead and gone,
The just, the fair, the gifted,—on whose graves long,
    grass hath grown.
With each scene of grace, or strain of power, or
    deed of high emprise,
Quick thoughts of some who loved them, unto my
    spirit rise;
And though dead, or never more to meet, a hallowed
    radiance bends,
Where to our earthly sight went down our unforgotten
    friends.

Our friends were seldom great or wise, in the
    world's fame or power;—
Oft lowly roofs warm hearts have nursed; high
    thought, and generous lore;

'Neath mountain slopes, in lone green vales, where
    tranquil wisdom dwelt,
We found them, learnt by heart their worth, their
    partial kindness felt.
And since,—as friends deemed those whose voice
    for Truth or Nature spoke;
Whose radiant thought, unselfish deed, some loftier
    impulse woke,
Like grand old books. And those whose song to
    life a brightness lends,
Though far apart,—unseen on earth—we ever
    deemed our friends.

With our old pleasures, there comes back, a bright
    and genial throng!—
Without them,—winter were too deep—and summer
    then, too long;—
Those days of wandering weary—through woods,
    o'er lake and fell;
By winding rivers' tangled banks, or fairies' moss-
    grown well.
Mute too, had been the wild old tales, at eve we
    would rehearse,
The legend quaint, the mirthful song, and soul-
    awakening verse.
From the days when primrose-gathering, we roamed
    in meadows fair,
To our later search in fields of thought, for flowers
    discovered there;

E'en joy unshared, was dull and dark, as a gem
    that dwelleth lone,
In some cavern, where no kindling ray hath e'er
    upon it shone.

What is our Faith? 'Tis but the trust in our
    Almighty Friend;
The substance of our brightest hopes when this
    dream of Life shall end;
When, Him whose glorious "form is Truth," as the
    gifted Heathen told—
Whose "shadow on the Earth is Light," the faithful
    shall behold.
And Heaven, that many-mansioned home, seems
    yet more bright and fair,
That the early lost we hope to find,—all perfect,—
    gathered there.
Where foes and falsehood are not, where pains and
    partings end,—
The home—the glorious home of Him, our Father
    and our Friend.

TO THE PACK-HORSE BELL
OF HARTSIDE.

Oft as thy silent rest I break,
 Thou relic of the hardy past !
Thy murmurs mountain echoes wake,—
 The rude dim life, and roaring blast,—
Of old laborious days, when men
 By simple strength and will o'ercame
Earth's barriers drear : and Commerce then,
 Dawned on those wilds no power could tame.
Spent fires, and wealth, hid far below
The bare, bleak fells, oft crowned with snow.

And thou, survivor of that band
 Of immemorial pioneers !
Round thy dusk form a radiance bland,
 Lights up the vista of the years,
When the staunch pack-horse gang of yore
 The Fell's unbroken rigours faced,

With stores for miners 'mid the moor.—
The Dane's stronghold at ten miles passed ;*
Then up the steeps their burden bore,
For trackless, treeless, ten miles more.

And o'er the trusty leader's crest
  Thou, vagrant bell ! a sphere wast hung ;
With chink through which storms never prest,
  Nor snows could still thy rolling tongue.
Long years, while loftier bells told clear
  Of bridals, burials, and war,
Through the bleak wilderness thy cheer
  Rang like a Prophet's voice afar :
Herald of peace, to clear the ways,
For mightier powers of modern days.

In no ignoble strife, to aid
  Those lowly wrestlers with the Fell ;
Through storms, and Helm-wind's gloomy shade,
  The demons, haply, to repel.†
And year by year, at winter's close,
  To meet the sunrise, through the dark,
Thy ringing peal up Hartside rose,
  Like carol of the morning lark :
In storm or calm, of equal cheer,
A voice of hope—a joy to hear.

* Melmerby—said to have been named from Melmor, one
of the three sons of Halfdan a Dane, who before the Norman
conquest, seated himself here, under the edge of the east
fells.

† Bells were anciently used as a safeguard against evil spirits.

When the staunch troop, with travel sore,
    Passed up within the Helm-cloud's veil,
And 'scaped the blast—yet heard its roar,
    Below, in many a western dale ;—
When they, to crown the march severe,
    Defiled through summits bleak and brown ;—
With sudden speed, and louder cheer,—
    Came clattering down to Alston town,
Round which the wide fells darkly peer,
    And grasping Winter cheats the year ;

Of snows dissolved, and opened ways,
    Round Cross-fell's base, they brought the tale;
Of all the promise of spring days,
    And produce of the Eden's vale.
Borne on light breeze, thy music brief
    Pleased wild bees murmuring 'mid the ling ;
Scarce startled fell-flocks, in their heaf,*
    By peak, lown† beck, or sievy spring ;
Or prompted moor-bird's faltering flight,
To wile the passing traveller's sight.

As thou—ne'er loftiest minster bells
    Rang in such day-spring radiance, spread
Swift o'er the vast, dark, solemn fells ;
    Nor out—such glorious evening red ;

* *Heaf,* that part of a mountain pasture to which a particular flock of sheep attaches itself. *Hevd,* Dan. prescriptive right.

† *Lown,* O.N. and Dan. sheltered. *Sievy, rushy,* siv. D. a rush.

As that descending pilgrims scanned,
　Which gilded oft the peaks and streams,
Of counties far beyond the land
　Of lakes, and fells, and poets' dreams;
The border land of raid and fray,
At peace, 'neath autumn's kindling ray.

And, prompt, in presage of the storm,
　Or, when the way grew rougher, steeper,
More clamorous grew thy voice—and warm- -
　To rouse the laggard and the sleeper.
In deepening seasons' gloom, the while,
　'Neath sudden storms with peril rife,
Thy voice led on the straggling file,
　Through hours of fearful stouran drife;*
'Mid blinding gloom a saving spell,
Wert thou,—heroic, nameless bell !

To lost ones, 'mid the wild fell's shroud,
　Or fog-lights-lured,—thy peal hath said,—
" Courage ! arise, and cry aloud ;—
　There yet is hope and human aid ! "
What joy, by many a hearth, there thrills
　The watchers for the lost ones back,

* Whirling, blinding, thick snow storm. *Drife* is not found
in any English collection of words. O. Norse, *drifa*—snow
fog. *Stour* may be the Scandinavian adjective *Stor*—great,
which is also used in Scotland ; or if *Stour*—dust in motion,
it is rather like tautology.

When first thy cheer rang down the hills,—
    Though snows and darkness closed the track ;—
Heard faint 'mid howling tempest's gloom ;
Or thunder-peals like crash of doom.

All this—but not his name, can'st show—
    That stern Columbus of the Fell ;
The master-mind, whose impulse, thou
    And that brave steed obeyed so well.
What of the staunch sure-footed horse—
    That all the mountain strife withstood,—
Trod straight—where none could see the course—
    Breasting the snowdrift and the flood?
Ah ! years o'ergrew their place and name,
That scathed not thy enduring frame !

Art spans the heights so lone and wide,
    And Science like a bird now soars ;
And eastern traffic's cheering tide,
    Steam through the miser region pours.
Still true—thou speak'st of heroes older,
    Whose toils have smoothed this world of ours;
Unconscious, resolute, and bolder,
    'Gainst Nature's unknown, awful powers.
Meetly, their dirge thou ringest now;—
The fells their cairn, enwreathed with snow.

NOTE.

This bell is known by tradition to have been hung over the collar of the leader of the Pack-Horse gang, which, at the close of the last century, twice a week crossed the fell from Penrith to Alston. It is of the usual metal, of very good workmanship, with the letters W. & R. on opposite sides of the open circle at the bottom, but neither name nor date could be recovered concerning it. In form and substance— its weight being 12 oz.—it is as unlike the toy bells sometimes seen on the necks of horses of the south of England, as its sonorous ring is to their lively jingle.

People of the last generation used to speak of the procession of pack-horses passing through Edenhall and Langwathby. A lady of 85 has a dim recollection of "three pack-horses going up Edenhall brow," when she lived there, before her seventh year; but that must have been in the decline of the traffic. When it began, the route to Alston was probably by a road over Penrith Fell, near the race course, to the old bridge between the two Salkelds—by Glassonby and Gamelsby, and the old road over Hartside, a lower portion of the fell. The more direct road might be much later than the building of Langwathby bridge; before which (1682) the Lang Wath must have been too formidable a barrier to be approached from a distance; not only from the usual current of the Eden, but from its liability to sudden overflow, so near the junction with Eamont, whenever westerly winds swept down Ullswater.

In Burn and Nicolson's History, there is a long list of the numbers of "Gangs of Pack-Horses" to and from Kendal; to London, and many other towns; to illustrate the extent of the woollen trade—the number of journeys weekly, and of

horses in each gang being given—"before the making of roads,"
after 1752. But no such traffic is mentioned in this direction,
though at that date (1777) there could have been little other
means of reaching Alston. And probably there were smaller
and earlier gangs, than any from Penrith ; from the fell-side
villages, where tradition of them is still rife. It is known to
have been impossible to make an ordinary pack-horse pass
before its leader. And doubtless from very early times, and
such responsibilities as these, we have a name expressive of
excellence in a horse, which is still common in our rural
districts ; and also, I hear, in Lincolnshire. However it
may be superseded, or be deemed homely or vulgar from later
associations, *Kappi*, was the Old Norse word for a hero : and
to cap is still to excel.

In Hodgson's History of Northumberland, it is said that
"the town of Alston is 20 miles from Penrith, 20 from
Brampton, and 23 from Hexham ; pent in a narrow valley
over which the mountains frown with a melancholy sterility."
Alston Moor is a wild, high parish, nine miles by eight ; of
dark moors intersected by streams and narrow valleys, in
some of which there is good pasturage. Since the making of
new roads to Penrith and Brampton, for which an Act of
Parliament was passed in 1823, the district is much improved
by cultivation and commerce ; and Alston has now its Floral
and Agricultural Shows.

The bell belonged to Miss Parley but
was after her death sent I believe
by me Dolls to the Museum
in Carlisle C P

THE DOVE.

WRITTEN DURING THE SIEGE OF PARIS. 1870.

When from the sad earth's deluged face
    The Lord's voice bade the waters cease,
Thou, Dove ! first brought'st to man the leaf
    Of Promise and of Peace.
And in the early Grecian days,
    When beauty claimed thee, gentle Dove !
Oft thou hast sped from isle to isle,
    Ambassador of Love.

Thy part was then less sad than now,
    Through War's and Famine's jaws to bring–
When man's swift transit-means were barred—
    Minutest scrolls beneath thy wing.
Joy to the sad beleaguered crowd,
    Where heart and hope began to fail,
When thou hast gleamed athwart the gloom,
    With news of hearts beyond the pale.

Through ages of the world unchanged,
   Thou breath'st an atmosphere above
Man's wars, and woes, and treacheries,—
   Own'st but the instinct of thy love.
'Mid slaughter brave; 'mid ruin true;
   Unweeting States', or Kings' decree,
No worldly wile, or power can warp
   The Dove's divine simplicity.

POSTSCTIPT. *June*, 1871.

What means, meek Dove!—in idlesse gay,
   When all is calm by land and sea,—
That men, when war, nor wild-chace call,
   Have turned their cruel rage on thee?

Know they, whose laws forbid the sport
   In great beasts' agonies to deal,
That pangs of each torn lingering dove
   Are keen as baited monsters feel?

Yet pain, or death thus multiplied,
   In selfish man no pity moves;
And Fashion and Frivolity
   Applaud a hecatomb of Doves.

THE MOOR—ENCLOSED. 1850.

Dark Moor! Thy regal robe is torn ;—
  Daily thy face becomes more strange :
A lion tamed—a giant shorn—
  These types to me bespeak thy change.

I tread the old familiar ground,
  My course prescribed 'twixt lines of stone ;
And to the eye, or ear, its bound
  Gives scarce one well-known sight or tone.

Let Wisdom, Toil, and Enterprise,
  Fitly, enjoy thy wealth to be ;
Sweet memory of the Moor o'erlies,
  For me, this new fertility.

Though woods may wave, and grass may grow,
  Where only turf and moss have grown,
And Cultivation's magic show
  Harvests on hills of sand or stone.

I have its picture, perfect yet,
  Nor parted, seamed, or ploughed its face ;
Its wild rude charms I ne'er forget,
  Its wide old bounds, in thought, I trace.

Its denizens, all wild and bare,
  Still o'er the turfy hillocks sweep ;
A herd of lawless ponies there,
  Here straggling, predatory sheep.

Though gipsies camp, and vagrant herds
  Forever banished, or restrained ;
The very bees, and moorland birds,
  Forsake a region tilled and drained.

Yet Memory not alone retains
  The heathery hill, and vagrant track ;
But peoples, as of old, those scenes,
  And conjures thoughts and feelings back.

I see the lapwing-haunted pool,
  Though corn or grass has clothed its face ;
And feel again the sunset's cool,
  Of vanished summers on my face.

And watching that lone wailing bird,
　　Its wiles to lure me from its nest ;
Think how like our own wiles, to guard
　　Our highest joys from vulgar quest.

Recal the bridge, where I would dream,
　　At evening, o'er the moorland brook ;
Gaze up, or down the tide, and deem
　　On Hope or Memory I could look.

Flowers, leaves,—as life's events in march,—
　　Came on the clear advancing waves,
Like Hope and Youth—down past the arch—
　　Seemed sunsets, memories, and graves.

How mused, o'er old fights on the heath,
　　Or, treasure buried in the ground ;
And on the ancient grave, beneath
　　The lonely, unsuspected mound.

Dear friends, and dead, again I greet,
　　There see perpetual blooming flowers ;
Lost voices, words, and fragrance sweet,
　　May oft be there at evening hours.

My moorland picture keeps for age
  Some spell of Nature—cultureless,—
As green sod in the skylark's cage,
  Or towns-folks' bit of wilderness.

O, gleam above life's flickerings faint!
  O boon, by God's benign decree!
No art with power like theirs can paint—
  The Masters—Hope and Memory!

1870.

E D E N .

Amid Westmeria's uplands barren,
  Oft when the southern breezes blow,
From out the ancient wild-boar's warren
  There sounds a rattling fell-beck's flow.
As a fair child in stature growing,
  In that pure stream the vales rejoice ;
But calmer is its onward flowing,
  Than that early Eden's voice.

We heed not wail of sage prophetic,
  That fitting theme of song is o'er ;
Nor join the dirge of the poetic,
  Upon old Eden's golden shore.
Ages to come shall find unspent,
  Dear stream! thy power—thy beauty—fame,
In all thy course beneficent,
  And in the magic of thy name.

The dreamers of some blest ideal,
    O'er earth, one utt'rance only claim,
That life, beyond the stern and real,
    Breathes in the music of thy name.
And with its echoes' far vibration,
    Which ages—first to last—prolong,
Some bard may find meet inspiration
    To sing thee in harmonious song.

TO THE STEAM-PLOUGH

IN CAITHNESS. 1873.

Giant of later days ! benignly going,
Unchecked o'er fastnesses and deserts wild,
Abroad the seeds of peace and plenty throwing,
To the far North-sea, like a sportive child.

Beneficent enchanter ! 'neath thy power
Deserts primeval to new life are born ;
And in thy footsteps spring up herb and flower,
The fattening grasses, and the blessed corn.

The stern earth yields her fulness, at command
Of Science, messenger of God for human uses ;
Softens the hardness of the loftier land,
And frees, or turns to sap its marish juices.

Grim pioneer of man's best life we deem thee.
Where deer and wild-fowl held their lonely reign;
We cannot see beyond—but now esteem thee
Last triumph of the art of Tubal Cain.

At true Nobility's impulse, most noble,
Giving the landless land, the hungry bread;
Wiser than for wide space, or sport ignoble,
To drain the realm of faithful lustihed.

And in the roll of Nobles' lives and labours,—
When Scotia proudly counts her patriot band,—
Blessings of God, of peace, and of his neighbours,
Shall greet the name of noble Sutherland.

TO MY PURPLE BEECHES.

A greenwood influence around me dwells :—
Blithe birds and varying breeze—
Bounding my world,—your waving, rustling spells,
    O, great and gracious trees !
In ever-waxing breadth of bole and crown,
    With yearly heavenward reaches,
Extended shade, and earth-grasp deeper down,—
    Majestic Beeches !

In Summer's purple—Autumn's gold—ye stand,
    Aeriel sanctuaries ;
A beauty and a blessing in the land,
    O, great cathedral trees !
Oft, with small burthens of the day opprest,
    When languor Peace beseeches,
Fain, like the birds, I flee away to rest,
    In thought, within the Beeches.

In sleepless hours I hear a thousand birds,
  Within your arches dim,—
Ere day awakes out-lying flocks and herds,—
  Singing their morning hymn.
And from your depths, at sunset bright—those voices,
  Whose worship plainly teaches,
That every small bird in God's day rejoices,
  And in o'ershadowing Beeches.

Not trees of immemorial growth, indeed,
  Wearing historic glory;
But, like the ancients, beechen books I read,
  For solemn Truth and Story.
Memorials ever—wardens by the portal!
  Of Love and Goodness gone;
From earthly shadows to the life immortal,
  By you, still beckoning on!

Your voice through leafy Summer—singing, sighing,
  In Autumn hoarsely preaches;
Of Death and Doom, of golden pomp low-lying,
  'Neath ravaged naked Beeches,
Like some great-hearted Patriots—rich and free,—
  Beneficent to all;
As they who occupy large space should be,—
  Ye shelter great and small.

For passers by the small birds know no fear,
  In the great friendly trees ;
For school-boys, sportsmen,—harmless, saunt'ring
    near ;—
  None are their enemies.
And lessons from the birds man well may learn,
  God's times to meet with gladness ;—
They see their lofty halls, their shelter torn,
  Without a wail of sadness.

A feeble feathered folk !—yet wise withal ;
  Them Heavenly Wisdom teaches,
That He doth care for, and will shield them all,
  When Winter strips the Beeches.
" A lowlier home they'll seek, 'neath ivy leaves "—
  So I o'erhear their speeches ;—
" In hollow trees—'neath stacks' or cottage eaves,
  When storms assail the Beeches."

" Yet here, bright morns and eves, their songs will
    raise,—
  For none their right impeaches,—
Since, by the house in its deserted days,
  Their sires first found the Beeches."
O, fearful soul ! Leave all to God, in faith,
  As His own Spirit teaches ;
And pray—but for His rest, when thou, in Death,
  Shalt pass—beyond the Beeches.

SUMMER.

JUNE, 1873.

Genial June once more is o'er us,
    Rich in verdure, foliage, flowers ;
Rustling trees, and song-birds' chorus,
    Balmy airs and long bright hours.

With the beeches, dark, embowering,
    Blends laburnum's golden rain,*
Legend-hawthorn redly flowering,
    With lilac clusters come again.

Hills long bare 'neath winter's rigour,
    Now are joyous like the vales ;
In the verdure, life, and vigour,
    Born of genial skies and gales.

---

* "Gold regen ! Das gold regen !" was the continual
exclamation of a German gentleman travelling in the Isle of
Wight, in May. The name is as beautiful as appropriate —
golden rain.

Poetic May ! the chill deceiver;
　With windy brightness boding woe,
To hungry flocks ; a grudging giver
　To the grazing herds below.

Insect life, with hum now filling
　All the air, cold May represt;
Birds half starved—now ceaseless trilling,
　In the glow of June are blest.

For the long-immured, escaping
　To the Summer's haunts once more,
Heart and thought quick dreams are shaping,
　All that dwelt in them of yore.

Freshness brings back years of childhood,
　Warmth, old friends of fervent truth ;
Scents, recal the birken wild-wood,
　And the fragrant fields of youth.

Flowers of long-past years are blooming,
　Old vigour rustles in the breeze,
Undertones yet bees are booming,
　To old sylvan melodies.

Gales of Mercy, softly blowing.
   Earth's voices fitly in accord,
With rivers bright—in bounty flowing,
   Sing—For Summer Praise the Lord!

A TALE OF LATE OCTOBER.

Harvest is past, and cold and dull,
  The lingering Autumn's sun at noon ;
The barns and barnekins are full,*
  In slumber 'neath the hunters' moon.

Along the bounteous Eden's vale
  Plenty and rustic peace abound ;
At evening firesides song and tale,
  With busy wheels, go cheerful round.

What sough is that upon the breeze?
  Those sounds confused,—that measured fall?
Not helm-wind wrestling with the trees ;—
  A week agone it stripped them all.

* *Barnekin*, the outermost ward of a castle, within which
were the barns, stables, and cowhouses.

The good-man, listening, stepped without,
  Glanced round his garner'd, folded things ;
" 'Twill be a border raid, I doubt—
  That's Scotsmen's tramp the north-wind brings !"

"Ah ! no !"—said the foreboding mother,
  Pallid with vague unspoken fears ;—
For Age and Childhood grief to smother,
  She bravely strives with falling tears.

"Are not the waths* all watched and warded,—
  All that the rievers dare to take ?
Are not with dogs the passes guarded,
  And the stout watchers all awake ?"

But then, shot up from Penrith Fell,
  The beacon-flame ;—and Orton Scar,
And many a lone height blazed—to tell
  Swift tale of dread to vales afar.

Then trembling haste in homes to hide
  What each one loved and treasured most ;
While, like the Solway's rolling tide,
  Comes on the hungry riever-host.

* *Wath* is the popular word for *ford*.

Soon,—shriek, and prayer, and threatening hoarse,
Tell of assault, resistance, woe ;
But useless, rage—o'er-mastered force,—
To check the fierce unequal foe.

Morn dawns on waste, and fire, and death,
While flocks and herds are driven away,
By lonely moor, and darkling path,
To reach the border—if they may.

Sorrow and graves—home desolation,
For Winter's pinch—left in their track ;—
And, trace of swift retaliation,
They say is left in Dead Men's Slack.*

---

* At Lazonby is a field so named, popularly believed to
have been the burial place of some over-taken and unfortunate
party of marauding strangers.   It lay long undisturbed, and
when but lately its cultivation was begun, the remains of
bones, etc., disinterred, seemed to justify its traditional fame.
The succession of these scenes for many centuries, on both
sides the Border. make it impossible to fix on any date for
events of which the general features were so similar, and so
disastrous.   But no testimony to the truth of history and
tradition is more to be depended on than such old field-names.
Douglas Ing is still known by its old name, as was stated in
the Penrith Herald not long since.
"At the south end of the old bridge at Hoff, near Appleby.
is a field which in Mr. Machell's time was called Douglas
Ing ; where a battle was fought between the Scotch and
English : at which time Appleby was burned.   Bones have
been dug up near the old bridge stead.   Perhaps this may

Those days are gone—their echoes mute ;
    One people now, those foes of yore ;—
The ravage, blood-shed, hot pursuit,
    And stern reprisal,—come no more.

When we for Plenty thank the Lord,
    For harvests fair, and earth's increase,
O ! let thanksgivings deep be poured,
    For earth's best blessing—household Peace !

refer to the 13th Richard II., in which year, in the month of
November, when the Englishmen's barns were full, and their
yards or barnekins well stored for the winter, the Scots under
the conduct of the Earl of Murray and the Lord Douglas,
entered England and burnt the country of Gilsland, kept on
their journey to Brough under Stanemore, and so through
Westmorland and Cumberland ; and after much spoil and
waste in all the parts aforesaid, with many prisoners and
great riches, they returned to their own country."—*Drake's
Hist. Anglo Scotia. Burn & Nicolson's Westmorland*, p. 330.

Refers to death + burial of Venture of her sister Jane Farley

THE FUNERAL PSALM.

The village church was met for prayers
  In Sunday evening's brooding calm ;
And many an eye was dim with tears,
  As rose the solemn funeral psalm.

No sign within the still churchyard
  Of recent death, that strain to claim ;
No new made grave, no broken sward,
  No knell, no utt'rance of a name.

Enduring memory keeps in view
  The stragglers from that ancient fold :
Four hundred miles away, they knew
  She died, for whom the tear-drops rolled.

The knell scarce heard 'mid cities' roar,
  Far vibrates 'twixt the quiet hills,
As with its solemn, softening power,
  One death all hearts with sadness fills.

More sad that far away she lies,
  Where hers is called a stranger's grave,—
The friend of all—though 'neath soft skies
  There laurel bright, and cypress wave.

O'er name and dust, afar, they bend,
  But here, too, on the household stone,
Her name and loving memory blend
  With theirs of generations gone.

Dear Sister ! if the dead can hear,—
  Pure souls loved spots on earth can see—
That memory is the fame most dear,
  That psalm the requiem best for thee.

I may not grudge thy blessed lot ;
  But, till that psalm for me shall rise,
Colder the earth where thou art not,—
  Thy faith, hope, love's lost ministries !

8

THE HEAF ON THE FELL.*

No Domesday record tells
Of fastnesses and fells,
Blue lakes and grassy dells,
Carved out for courtier's meed, or for daring
    warrior's spoil ;
Long, Viking barks had swept
North seas, and while men slept,
Haply, fierce chiefs had leapt
Ashore, and in their fashion rude, ta'en seizin of the
    soil.

Ages of fierce unrest,
Not for mere Battle's zest—
Weak people backward prest
Fresh hordes ; who fain in fell-side homes their
    wanderings would cease ;

* *Heaf*, that part of an open fell pasture on which a
particular flock of sheep feeds, and becomes attached to.
Dan. *hævd*, prescriptive right. Icelandic, *hefda*.

Their sons, a stalwart band,
Maintained with the strong hand,
Their days long in the land ;
Their strength, their weapons, words of war, turned
to the life of peace.

No conqueror drove forth,
From th' old unquiet North,
Its moist skies and upland earth,
Those stern and hardy settlers, from out their quiet
tillage ;
When all with blood was dark,
No mandate came t' empark   .
The lofty, bleak out-mark ;
Joint remnant, and firm right, of many an ancient
fell-side village.

Ages of summer days,
There flocks are wont to graze ;
Each o'er its own heaf strays,
Like some Arcadian peoples, undivided, yet apart ;
Scarce heeding helm-wind's shocks,
Fronting in force, the fox,
And sheltering 'neath the rocks,
While o'er their varied pastures tempests roll, and
lightnings dart.

Nought there but peaceful things,—
Pure airs, and infant springs,
The atmosphere that flings
Such glory o'er the mountain-heads, and slopes so
    near the skies ;
    And, flocks that dwelt below
    Heard screaming moor-birds crow,
    And brattling fell-becks flow,
But nought to mar the quiet of that pastoral paradise.

The wild bees early came,
Their sweet first-fruits to claim,
When whins were all aflame,
Telling far up the heights, the immemorial summer
    story ;
    Rifling, with victor-boom,
    The honey-rife ling-bloom ;
    Coming soon-laden home,
When autumn clad the fells in a soft haze of purple
    glory.

'Neath the last hedge's frieze,
Too, hives of garden bees,
Brought within scent of these,
The Northern summer's latest, richest yielding
    flowers ;

Transported, pillion-tied,
By night, like stolen bride,—
Swarm forth at morning—wide,
To bring their latest gatherings in from the fragrant
moors.

O, lovely mountain heaf !
Oft scene of pastoral grief,
Dire, keen, though haply brief,
When envious neighbours over their viewless
boundaries prest ;
Or barking collies sent,
To hound from off the bent
Sheep of such old descent,
From that familiar spot which was their chosen
home and rest.

Ah, suffering, silly sheep !
Almost with you I weep,—
I share your yearning deep ;
Your wrongs and scattered wretchedness, proclaimed
afar, I know.
Forced flight to rocks and bogs,—
O'er the crag's brink in fogs—
The terrors of the dogs,
And all the helpless little lambs', and wrecklings'
overthrow.

But what are griefs like yours?—
Free to bleat among the moors—
To those which man endures?
With his deep thoughts; and far, and oft, reflected
memories,—
Quivering at music's tone—
From generations gone,
Heaping up woes upon
The heads of ruined folk, in ruthless War's
extremities.

At cruel kings' behest,
Whole peoples dispossest
Of all they loved the best;
Their slaughtered sons,—their ravaged lands,—their
pleasant homes upbroken ;—
Their Fathers' faith and fame,
Their ancient country's name,—
Its tongue—O, Tyrant's shame !
Only in secret sorrow, or in exile to be spoken.

Little they care or wot,
Whose own the sheep are not,
The misery they allot;
But yet shall the Good Shepherd come, some day,
and rede the wrong;

And such kings shall wrath endure,
When our Lord shall, stern, abjure
The oppressors of the poor;
And, haply, range on His right hand, those crushed
on earth so long.

1872.

NOTE.

It may be difficult to convey to a stranger an idea of the
boundless sheep-ranges of our Northern fells, unless he should
have stood and looked from the top of Helvellyn or Cross
Fell; if so, and he can recal the dark tumultuous wastes
stretching away to the horizon on every side, he will have an
idea of the undivided fell-pastures of several parishes, (from
the first of these heights he will see little else,)—but not of
the numbers of interests, and flocks there mingled—at large,
yet separate—nor of the extent to which the instinct of the
sheep to keep to their own heaf, is calculated on, as one of
the safe-guards of such property.—*From a Paper on "Heaf,"
in Notes and Queries, M., Jan. 18th,* 1873.

The right of pasturage on the parish waste, of owner or
occupier, is strictly proportioned by the in-field land he holds;
and is kept up by continued use. The rule is, to keep as
much stock on the fell in summer, as his enclosed land will
maintain in winter.

EDEN'S STORY.

Not of far Eastern life or glory,
　　Not of soft Paradisal bowers,
Seemeth to me that chiming story,
　　Eden tells through quiet hours ;
But like an ancient bard descending,
　　Striking on his silver strings,—
Eden through the valleys wending,
　　Of forgotten Northmen sings.

Echoes Arthurian may 'waken,
　　As flowing by Pendragon's hold ;
By stately pile and halls forsaken,
　　Faint sound of horn of baron bold.
But Northmen's trophy none discovers ;
　　They might have perished, root and branch,
Those resolute, home-seeking rovers,—
　　Those ceaseless Vikings—fierce and staunch :

For aught of date, in History's pages,
  For certain trace, in temple—tomb.
No sculptures theirs—as through long ages—
  Earth keeps in memory of Rome.
Yet here their footsteps earth hath shown,
  Impressed on England's morning dew ;
As if, of wanderers ere the dawn,
  O'er meadows green and mountains blue.

No dream that in the air remaineth,
  That Danish voice the shepherd hears ;*
Where mead, and grove, and rock retaineth
  Names each hath borne, a thousand years.

* Wordsworth. A Fragment. This poem, to which no
note is given, seems an embodiment of pervading local
tradition, as well as an allusion to the legend of the thraldom
of the cattle to the potent spell of harmony, which rings
through the air. as they listen to the Danish or Norseland
boy, sadly singing the old bardic lays over the barrows of his
forefathers.

> " A harp is o'er his shoulders slung,
>   He rests the harp upon his knee ;
> And there, in a forgotten tongue
>   He warbles melody.
> Of flocks upon the neighbouring hills
>   He is the darling and the joy ;
> And often, when no cause appears
> The mountain ponies prick their ears,
>   They hear the Danish boy.
> While in the dell he sits alone,
> Beside the tree and corner stone."

The burden of the Eden's song
　　Brings echoes of the Northern seas;
And oft, quaint rustic speech may throng
　　The thought with hints and memories,

Of storms and bloodshed;—strife the sorest—
　　When Northmen came in conquering mood;
Crashing like whirlwind through the forest,
　　As down their earliest paths they trod.
And how,—their way resistless, wrestling,—
　　Like Autumn's flood the vales they filled;
How, 'neath the fells, familiar, nestling,
　　Their homes they made, their fields they tilled.

Took kindly to the mists and storms;
　　And strove with ice and flinty earth,
And tempests, streams, and mountain forms,
　　They named as in the Higher North.
How kept of land and speech their hold,
　　And 'neath the hard gray fell-sides grew,—
While kingdoms changed, and ages rolled—
　　Those hard true Englishmen we view.

NOTE.

It cannot be doubted that familiarity with Westmorland speech must have influenced the tastes and deepest studies of Richard Cleasby, whose death a quarter of a century ago at Copenhagen, where he was engaged in the publication of his Icelandic and English Dictionary, was the grief of Northern scholars. For twenty years no one was found to complete the work, for which the materials were known to be of such excellence. It has lately been given to the world by the exertions of his family, assisted by the ablest Scandinavian scholars, and fostered by the University Press of Oxford. A noble monument to his memory, of which Westmorland is naturally proud. For though born in London, his father was born at Crag House, Stainmore, the family property; and country tradition preserves,—with Joseph Addison's father's house, and other matters of local interest,—how Stephen, after the early death of his mother, who was Miss Mary Wilson of Burtergill, near Warcop, lived much with her family, till he went to London, to his uncle, Richard Wilson, the founder of that mercantile Russia House to which he eventually succeeded, and to which, as to other northern houses, then, came repeated accessions from the same place and family.

Thus in early life, and till he finally left his father's house, Richard Cleasby must have been associated with natives of the north, who doubtless continued to use the idiomatic expressions which people of those counties so rarely leave off, whatever their pronunciation or after-education. And in his energetic character, the perseverance with which, under all discouragements, he pursued his great object—the study of languages—and in the direction of his studies to those Northern tongues, to which at that time so few southern English were attracted, there seems acknowledgment of the

* Icelandic English Dictionary. Based on M.S. Collection of the late Richard Cleasby. Enlarged and Completed by Gudbrand Vigfusson, M.A. Clarendon Press, Oxford, 1874.

unconscious early influences ; which, beyond circumstances of
birth or property, constitute the best ground on which to
claim Richard Cleasby as one of the sons of Westmorland.

These early impressions must have been deepened by visits
to the county at later periods ; and so it was no more
remarkable for him, a Londoner, to write to his brother from
Germany of a "raffish looking set"—than for Miss Wordsworth to write of "flowers growing on the riggins of Highland
cottages," and of a town "seeming to stand in a bottom."

The fresh interest to such an inquirer, familiar with the
names and speech of Upper Eden, on finding at Copenhagen,
forty years ago,—long before Professor Worsaae's visit to
England—Hellbeck, and Lund, and Kirkby, and all the
other *bys* and *dales*, again, we may imagine. As well as
many names for natural objects, fields, etc.; and many words
connected with storms, and old occupations. "At skarp en
hest," might have recalled the Westmorland expression, "At
sharp a horse," for the frost. How often, on Stainmore, he
must have heard of "stouren drife"—the expressive term for
a great snow-storm, still in use along the fell-sides of Westmorland, and of Upper East Cumberland, though apparently
unknown at Carlisle, or in books—save in the old Norse,
drifa—snow-fog. How interesting if he had lived to tell us,
as seems probable, that though it might have dropped out of
modern Danish, the old word survives in the speech of our
fells :—and whether the prefix is the consistent Scandinavian
adjective, *stor*—great, slightly modified, as in "*Den Store
Verden*"—the Great World.

For this, and many things in want of such authority, we
cannot help fearing that—though the loss dreaded to the
English language in the death of Richard Cleasby, may now
be made up by this excellent Dictionary—there must remain
a disadvantage to our dialect : to those words which have no
date nor history, but on which he might have shed light, from
both points of view, such as no one may be left to supply.

WAITING FOR THE DAY.

In the small hours past the midnight,
   Counting how the clocks are going;
In the gloom, or moonlight, voiceless,
   Save for early cocks a-crowing.
Oft I watch the bright stars speeding
   On their darkly radiant way;
Of the sleepless all unheeding,
     Waiting for the day.

Glad the sounds of earth's awaking!
   Welcome early, swift, foot-fall,
Or the gleam of passing lantern,
   Flashing on my chamber wall.
For the far off twinkling radiance,
   For the transient flashing ray,
Each are portions of the glory
     Waiting for the day.

O ! still small hours ! most eloquent
   Of th' Almighty's love and care ;
Of the faith and hope eternal,
   Of the privilege of prayer.
Songs in the night ! of wondrous music ;
   They that hear them by the way,
Self-forgetting, rest in patience,
   Waiting for the day.

THE LAST TREE OF INGLEWOOD FOREST.

TO A PICTURE FRAME.

Last tree of the forest—last oak of the wood !
That land-mark and umpire, six ages hath stood.
When the men of Carlisle came their boundary to
    ride,
'Twas to thee that they looked, o'er the moss, as
    their guide.
Apart,—not in ranks, with the chiefs of the wood,—
With his children around him, the patriarch stood.
And here is a relic,—a frame made of part
Of the old forest giant's unperishing heart ;
For a picture—but not of his tottering decay,—
Let us look on the oak in his flourishing day !
In that fibre so firm, in that frame polished bright,
There are streaks, as through branches, of sun's
    setting light.

A picture, methinks, looking through it, I see,
Of ages long gone, in the green-wood so free ;—
Sylvan strength, and rich leafage, and high-arching
       glades :
Moss, moorland, and tarn ;—rivers, rocks, and
       cascades.
And that tinting harmonious, in forests that weaves—
Green, golden, gray, russet—a glory of leaves.
A forest right royal, for a king to hold chase ;
Where the spoil of his bow was left thick on the
       place.

Now the chase is gone by—all the gallant pursuit—
Loud voices and far-sounding bugles are mute ;
The last rays of sunset stream in through the boughs,
And the deer-herds steal out, in the stillness, to
       browse,
In that greenness where cool dews till noontide had .
       lain,
And which moonlight discovers all sparkling again.

Perchance, ages ere this, as morn gleamed on the
       oak,
And from old Castle Hewen ascended the smoke,
Its tops waved salute to Tarn Wadling's lost pile,
While "King Arthur kept court in merry Carleil:"
When the stern forest depths but the boldest would
       trace,
And of wolf, or of wild-boar was often the chase.

And, later, when outlaws through famed "Englyshe
    Wood,"—
Adam Bell and his fellows, those archers so good,—
Ranged, and hunted the deer, spite of monarchs'
    decree,
Was their banquet and rest beneath this "trusty
    tree"?
Which o'er wastes, long unstable, its green flag hath
    swayed,
As oft hermit and way-farer slept in its shade;
Hath seen armies pass onwards, to battle and scath;
And monarchs—in triumph, in bonds, or in death.
Hath outcasts and wanderers screened from the
    blast;
And wreaths o'er the fallen, in secret hath cast.

Yes, landmark and chronicle, peaceful old tree!
Time fails to recount all thou pictur'st to me;—
How, through ages of strife, in a war-weary land,
Like a great rock of refuge the old oak would stand;
Friend and guide, through the ages, that all men
    could trust!
And its memory is sweet—like the fame of the just.

And long in our homes, we may reverently look,
On branches of Inglewood's last forest oak,
Adorning the walls—or protecting the store
Of choice things—of relics—of records—and lore;
When war, raid, and ravage are heard of no more.

NOTE.

"On Wragmire Moss, until 1823, there was a well-known oak, known as the last tree of Inglewood Forest, which had survived the blasts of 700 or 800 winters. This time-honoured oak was remarkable not only for the beauty of the wood, which was marked in a similar manner to satin wood, but as being a boundary mark between the manors of the Duke of Devonshire and the Dean and Chapter of Carlisle, as also between the parishes of Hesket, and St. Cuthbert's, Carlisle ; and was noticed as such for upwards of 600 years. This gnarled and knotted oak, which had weathered so many hundred stormy winters, was become considerably decayed in its trunk. It fell not, however, by the tempest or the axe, but from sheer old age ; on the 13th June, 1823.* If not of late years, as beautiful in its foliage, nor presenting such a goodly assemblage of wide-spreading and umbrageous branches as some other celebrated oaks, yet it was an object of great interest, being the veritable last tree of Inglewood Forest. Xerxes, who cared not for the sacrifice of human life, would not suffer his army to destroy trees, and halted his mighty host for three days that he might repose beneath the Phrygian plane ; and yet, perhaps that tree had not numbered half the years of this relic of Inglewood, under whose spreading branches may have reposed the victorious Edward I., who is said to have killed 200 bucks in this ancient forest, and perhaps, at a later period, "John de Corbrig, the poor hermit" of Wragmire, has counted his beads beneath its shade.

* "It is not a little remarkable that on the same day on which this ancient tree fell, Mr. Robert Bowman, of Irthington, a patriarch of 118 years, departed this life."

"The great north road through Carlisle to Edinburgh and Glasgow traverses this parish (of Hesket), and passes over Wragmire Moss, of which part of the road we have the following notice in Bishop Nicolson's MSS. :—'In 1354 a grant was made of forty days' indulgence to any that should contribute to the repairs of the highway, through Wragmire : and to the support of John de Corbrig, a poor hermit living in that part.'"—*Jefferson's History of Leath Ward.*

Relics of the wood of this fine old oak, are preserved in many homes of Cumberland people. In forms of cabinet, sideboard, bookcase, and picture-frames.

THE WELCOME EAST-WIND. 1872.

I heard long sound of southern waters flowing,
 On wintry breezes borne ;
And saw, through dashing rains, the tree-tops blowing,
 Their splendours reft and torn.
Then Ullswater, with all her tribute flushing,
 Swept down by western gales,
Sends floods through Eamont's channel, northward
 rushing,
 O'er Eden and her vales.

And spreading swift, o'er corn-lands,—meads low
 lying,
 Spurning her bridges' bounds—
Rolls Eden reckless—frightened creatures flying,
 To reach the higher grounds.
And full and frantic go the little rivers,
 As men in drunkards' plight,
That in their bounds were joy and plenty givers ;
 Joined in disastrous might.

Lands drenched, ploughs idle, homes oft damp and
    dreary,
    Flocks shivering in the mud ;
The East-wind comes to man and beast, rain-weary,
    Prompt harbinger of good.
The keen wind, "as it listeth," timely blowing,
    Dries up the watery vales ;
Th' Almighty's will in all its motions flowing,
    Whose mercy never fails.

AN INCIDENT OF EMIGRATION.

He left his land for lack of gear,
  His father's land, his new-won bride ;
In loss of health, for lack of care—
  Of love—afar the wanderer died.

He heard that she for whom he strove,
  Their babe—ere gold or home were made—
Passed from earth's pains, and parted love,
  And in a Scottish grave were laid.

O ! vainly parted ones ! of Gold,
  Of Earth, or Time, scant portion given ;—
But Scotia's scattered children hold,
  O'er all, the faith to meet in heaven.

DIALECT.

THE ECHOES OF OLD CUMBERLAND would be incomplete without the tones of its dialect; so ancient, and with local variations, still so widely spoken in rural districts. Most natives of the county must remember old persons who considered it a sort of disloyalty and affectation to use modern words in speaking, though they might be well enough acquainted with them in books. Where there are two terms for most things, it is natural to use that which will be best understood; and this may account for changes of expression which have been remarked on, in persons first addressing a native and then a stranger. It should be said that in Cumberland there are variations of speech, coming in for the most part, imperceptibly, which at the extremities of the county amount to a considerable difference of sound and accent; as in the word HOME, which at the Scottish border is *hame*, in the Carlisle district *heäme*, as written by Miss Blamire, in the country round Penrith *hyam*, and bordering Lancashire, *yam*. Of one change the locality is strictly defined: it is often remarked by country people that "It is *mine* an' *thine* at Lazonby, but *meyne* an' *theyne* at Kirkoswald." The two villages are on opposite banks of the Eden, not much more than a mile apart. Below this the definite article, which is abbreviated through upper and central Cumberland, and all over Westmorland, as in Yorkshire, comes into more general use, and the speech, northwards, grows more musical. These changes are quite in accordance with others of place and field-names thereabouts. In one half the county, words may be heard which are hardly known in the other; and we have some for which there is no single English equivalent. Strangers think the sound of our dialect harsh; but those who suppose it necessarily associated with ignorance, make a great mistake. Our first dialect writers, as Relph and Miss Blamire, were cultivated and refined people. Even now may sometimes be heard excellent discussions or observations on such subjects as "t' Rawman Rwoad," or "t' geological dip o' t' strata," in certain directions; which seem to show, that though new words must come in, they will be for some time longer, treated exactly like the old ones. Strangers would smile—their associations with the dialect may probably dispose them to do so,—since it has been so successfully used by Dr. Gibson, and others, as a medium for humorous writing. But it has far higher claims to respect than that; and the importance of preserving a faithful record of old provincial speech is now so generally recognized, that we do not so often hear of such persons as an eloquent advocate of dialects denounces.

> " The man who scorns and not respects
> Our England's rural dialects ;
> The man to whose dull ear and eye
> Their eloquent antiquity
> Seems nothing more than vulgar babble
> Of some uneducated rabble :
> Who will not see and ponder well,
> That every common syllable
> Is picturesquely crusted o'er
> With fancy and with metaphor ;
> And savours of the thoughts and ways
> Of simpler lives and fresher days ! "

Adding with much feeling—

> " Who, that is human, would not rise,
> And help the reverend and the wise
> By tenderest culture long to stay
> The sad inevitable day,
> When all that grace and all that lore
> Shall dwell in living speech no more?"
> From *Auld Lang Syne.*   By *Arthur Munby.**

In the following pieces it has not seemed necessary to alter the spelling of words so much as to lock up the sense from general readers. Those of the two counties, who know the dialect,

* *Verses Old and New.*   Bell and Dalby, 1865.

may be depended on for giving the vowels the due breadth of their old northern sound; *a* as aa, or au; *o*, as aw, in many words; *u*, and *ou*, as oo ; and for not mitigating the sound of *h*, and *r*; besides other peculiarities of Eastern Cumberland not so easily written as said.

The first dialect piece belongs to Upper East Cumberland—and adjoining part of Westmorland, as spoken at the date given, and even now, in many places. The three following are in the speech of North-East Cumberland; and the last that of the Northern Border, or lowland Scottish. There are no words which have not been heard in use since the dates given; but there may be a possible incon-sistency in the location of ings, where the definite article is used, *i. c.* below Kirkoswald.

DIFFERENCE OF OPINION

ABOUT OUR MUDDER TONGUE. 1850.

A grey-haired dweller of the dale
With his far-travelled friend, behold ;—
In converse calm, till difference rose,—
One lauds new things—one loves the old.

"You see, the railways, uncle, stretch
    Across the land, from town to town,
And equal privileges bring
    To spots like this—once drear and lone.

"They'll soften life's asperities
    In manners—customs—where they reach ;
We soon shall hear, the kingdom through,
    Smooth uniformity of speech."

"What! Do they think to larn fwok, aw—
To talk alike, aw England through?
Is Cummerland to throw away
    Auld words like ours, for sūm 'at's new?

"My certie !* but they're sair mista'en,
    'At think to grund us down sae flat!
We say our say,—an' pay our way,—
    Our-sels ;—we're owre far north for that!

"We read our Bibles, an' our buiks,
    Wi' aw our best pronunciation ;
But leavin' off our mudder-tongue
    At hyam, 's nae part of edecation.

"We mainly talk to finer fwok
    I' t' buik-wurds, put in for a bit ;
An' write an' spell t'em fast eneugh,
    But niver t' auld 'ans could forgit.

"A bonny stwory it wad be,
    If we forgat what t' auld fwok said !
Or thowt sham o' the'r wise auld words,
    As suin as iver they're low-laid.

* Pron. Sartie—my word for it.

"An' when we're sturr't,[1] owts deep, at heart,
  T' words spring we kent when we war young ;
If t' railways rive t' land aw to rags,
  They'll nut destroy our mudder-tongue.

"What's t' use o' speakin' unket[2] words,
  'At t' nags an' kye taks by contràrics?
An' t' heeght o' daftness it wad be,
  To bodder t' dogs wi' dixonàries.[3]

" Like yon fine farmer, com frac t' south,
  An' fand a dog sae wise an' clever ;
He thowt if he could nobbut buy't,
  'T wad seave him fash, wi' t' sheep, for iver.[4]

" But when he'd bowt it—nūt for him
  'T wad fetch or follow,—gedder—wheel ;—
It could n't tell a word he said,—
  T' puir dog ! 'at could ha' duin sae weel !

---

1 Stirred.   2 *Unket*—unfamiliar.
  3 *Dixonaries*—a term which used to be scornfully given to
long hard words ;—chiefly perhaps, to Latinized words,
which always sound like aliens in the dialect. "Dunnet thou
dictate !" was once said by a stranger to a native, who was
laying down the law, at a wrestling match, 60 years ago.
The answer amounted to, "Confound thy dictates ! Let's ha'
nin o' thy dixonaries here !" (Dictionaries.)
  4 *Fash for iver*—an infinite amount of trouble.

" It's useless,—an' it's nūt good manners,—
To talk to nowder men ner dogs
I' words they dunnet ūnderstand.—
Cūm, Laddie!* min†—fetch on,—wi' t' hogs!"‡

* *Laddie*—a common name for a sheep dog.
† *Min*—man.   ‡ *Hogs*—yearling sheep.

"I NIVER RUED BUT YENCE."

Nae time or service blunts the sense
   O' that auld heamly Cumbrian phrase,
Oft hard—"I niver rued but yence;"
   An' sometimes—"it was aw my days!"

Nor thousand minstrels o' remorse
   Hae fund yae form o' utterance,
In aw their sangs, o' deeper fworce
   Than this—I niver rued but yence.

The stracklin'* spends gude neame an' gear,
   His fwore-elders' inheritance,
Far back, for mony a hundred year;—
   An' niver—niver rues but yence.

      * *Stracklin'*—a spendthrift.

An' yon fause man—he's aund to rue,*
Through aw his warldly arrogance—
'At left his auld luive for a new:
    An' he—hes niver lo'ed but yence.

Oft graves hae clwosed ower wrangs unreeghted,
    An' wearin' thowts o' penitence,
Hae driven the wranger—heart-beneeghted—
    To 'sccape frae rue an' life at yence.

For darkest neeght, nor fair day-leeght,—
    Nae time o' year, nor change o' days,
Nae wind 'at blaws, that sufferer knows,
    That cloud ower life sall rive, or raise.

God help them that sae sairly languish!
    Greet hearts, they say, dree weird intense;
An' monarchs hev-n't 'sceaped the anguish
    O' deeds they niver rued but yence.

---

* *Aund to rue*—fated, doomed to remorse, regret. Perhaps
connected with *audna*—fate. Old Norse.

CUMBERLAND THANKSGIVING SONG.

MARCH 2ND, 1872.

The blast frae dark fells o'er us,
　　That sweeps through Cumbria's vales,
Taks up the nation's chorus,—
　　God bless the Prince o' Wales!
Wi' voice o' beacons bleezin',
　　Lown breeze owre muirs an' cairns,—
God bless our Danish Princess!
　　God bless their bonny bairns!

Wi' London millions pourin'
　　For thanksgivin' an' prayers,
"The Queen!"—"The Prince!"—implorin'
　　Blessin's on them an' theirs;
Thanksgivin'-Cumbrians gather—
　　For that spared royal life;
To the smaa bairns their father—
　　The husband to his wife.

10

Frae thousand years abidin',
'Mang fastnesses an' fells,—
Auld speech an' spirit guidin'—
The Danish outcome tells.
Amaist like lang-kent faces,
This heamly phrase oft pours
A spell o'er hearts o' dales-fwok,—
"Their fore-elders* an' ours!"

We grat—we joyed—for England!
Our Queen—our Prince—our prayers!
An' for our peerless Princess,
An' their reeght royal heirs!
We haud a double fealty,
Amang our fells an' cairns;—
God bless the twea auld kingdoms!
God bless the Royal bairns!

God save the Queen lang o'er us!
God save the Prince o' Wales!
This day's the Empire's chorus,
Wheas sunshine never fails.

---

* *Fore-elders*, in Cumberland, means ancestors generally,
not parents—as in Denmark.   It seems an indefinable but
powerful bond among warm-hearted and stationary people,
that their fore-elders were acquainted.   And at the time of
the Prince of Wales' marriage to the Princess of Denmark,
great joy was expressed by old country people, on this
account.   Neither time, nor wars of old, seem to interfere
with the feeling.

Wi' lofty beacons flashin',—
  Wi' deep sea's whispered tales,—
Wi' tower an' rampart crashin',—
  God bless the Prince o' Wales !

THE BROKKEN STATESMAN. 1850.

Aye, I yence was the heir,—though times hae
     changed sair—
O' that lown-liggin' onset[1] by fair Eden side ;
Aw its green holms an' ings,[2] whaur the furst o'
     gurse springs,
   An' yon rich hingin'[3] cworn-fields,—our fwore-
     elders' pride.
Aye me ! still, though it's lang, I mind weel o' the
     sang
   'At through my young heart, wi' sec bevers[4] wad
     thrill,
When a share on 't was mine, 'at I ne'er thowt to
     tyne,[5]
   It was " Canny auld Cummerland caps them aw
     still."

---

1 *Lown-liggin' onset*—a farm-house and outbuildings lying
in a sheltered situation.   2 *Ings*—meadows.   3 *Hingin*—
sloping.   4 *Bever*—to tremble, *bevers*—agitation.   5 *Tyne*—
to lose.

O, the fule rackle days ! when in wild outwart[1] ways,
I spent time but i' daftness, wi' raff an' expense.
Then the auld land's neglect, an' my friends' lost
respect,
While I scworned to tek counsel—I ne'er rued
but yence !
The fair heame I hed meade—wife an' bairns suin
low-laid—
Though she cannily said,—"Aye, he's warst till
his-sel ! "
But, through aw change an' chance I hae ne'er rued
but yence,
An' I hear a voice flyte[2]—waur ner ill-tongues[3]
could tell.

When drink hed browt sorrow—fresh money to
borrow,
Wi' deep debt o' the riggin,[4] puir crops o' the
hill ;
Wi' life at the barest, heart-sorrow fell sairest :
Yet e'en then, I thowt—Cummerland caps them
aw still.

---

1 *Outwart*—(much in use, but not in print)—dissipated,
irregular—perhaps degenerate, if from *Udart*, Dan. degenerate.   2 *Flyte* to upbraid, scold.   3 *Ill-tongues*—revilers,
detractors.   4 *Debt o' the riggin'*—mortgage on the property.

Fwok tell o' grand prairies, whaur rowth[1] without
    care is,
    Lands owre-sea, whaur gowd ligs by beck-side
      an' hill ;
An' pastures to feed on,—like auld ings by Eden ;
    But,—canny auld Cummerland caps them aw still !

Oft a shek o' the hand, frae my scuil-fellows grand,
    Whea come back i' their luck, gang as far as they
      will,—
Brings sad thowts to my mind, though their words
    may be kind,
    For we aw ken 'at Cummerland caps them aw still.
Gude forgie me the past ! The auld land's geane at
    last !
    An' for me, feal't an' feckless,[2] I'll lait nae new
      biel' ;[3]
But just six feet o' yerth, i' the land o' my birth,
    Whaur I'll lig, iv auld Cummerland, 'mang them
      aw still !

1 *Rowth*—plenty.
2 *Feal't an' feckless*—failed, fallen off and powerless.
3 *Lait nae new biel'* (bield)—seek no new shelter.

NOTE.

'Statesman—Estatesman, a yeoman, small land-owner ;
equal to laird in Scotland. The term may now be applied
to men of various means, habits, and education, as some have
become larger proprietors. But large or small—the independ-
ance, and love and enjoyment of their own *land*, is common
to all who have been accustomed to live on it.

Various causes have contributed to reduce the numbers of
these small properties in the two counties, and the coming
in of strangers, and laying together of large estates, precludes
the possibility of return to this old state of things. Though
"The Brokken Statesman" is a purely imaginary being, and
the date given is merely to indicate the time at which such a
style of expression might have been used, instances are sadly
numerous of decadence from similar causes. But the reduced
number of small properties is not all attributable to disaster.
Though some have declined, it should be remembered that
very many families have risen, by fortunate circumstances, by
successful enterprise or learning, above their old position ;
and their names are now found in other categories. In almost
every parish the two extremes may meet, and the old "scuil-
fellowship" be warmly acknowledged.

My Falthr was the last o' the ould
Slatesmen - farming his own Lan
R.P.

"TO SEE OURSELS AS ITHERS SEE US."

(BORDER DIALECT.)

"O ! wad kind heaven the giftie gie us,
To see oursels as ithers see us !"

Burns.

As time the bloom frae life is stealing,
  O ! let not Heaven the giftie gie us,—
Alien frae ither gifts and feeling,—
  To see oursels as ithers see us.
Kind folk, wi' sympathy that soothe
  Some sufferers' life o' lanely languor,
Might say, if they should find the truth,—
  That's just a sort o' Döppelganger.

Not o' that gruesome German kind,
  That flay folk out o' life and sense ;
But in twa places—form and mind,—
  At hame, and far abroad at yence.

While in th' accustomed nuik, perforce,
  Seeming to sit, wi' half-shut eyes,
In Thought's and Fancy's vagrant course
  Yen meets nae bars nor boundaries,

'Mid far, fair haunts o' Nature wand'ring ;
  And grand, auld, famous scenes may view ;
Or, in the groves o' Memory pondering,
  See sunset radiance blinking through.
They think life held on stern conditions,
  That ken o' laneliness and pain ;
But not o' lightsome gleams and visions
  Kind Heaven has mercifully gi'en.

While weakness clips not wings o' fancy,
  Nor wand'ring pains extinguish thought ;
And wi' a sort o' necromancy
  That tea-pot, sma' and dark, is fraught,
At evening hours :—I disagree
  For yence wi' Burns. Far happier wi' us
To mak' the best o' things that be,
  Not "see oursels as ithers see us."

TRANSLATIONS.

 FEW Translations of modern poems, chiefly Danish, are offered to the reader, in the hope that the manly and home-loving spirit of the northern poetry may still awaken an echo in the land which bears in language and institutions so many traces of the northern character.

ELSINORE.

FROM THE DANISH OF INGEMANN.

Roll, from the sea's depths, Stream profound!
Fill with thy song of waves the Sound!
Troops of blithe sailors hither float,
Sunshine on thousand wings is brought,
And billow-towers from far coasts driven,
Out-din the thunder-peals of Heaven.
They hail, amid the Cannons' roar,
The Danish Flag, the Danish Shore.

On the fair Coast, by the deep Sound,
Stands Abilgaard, and Rosenlund.
With field, and grove, and hill, looks down
Bordering the Stream, the quaint old town.
And Kronborg's stately Castle-Keep,
Lord of the Sound, towers o'er the deep;
And passing guns hail with accord
The Danish Flag, the Danish Lord.

Through the World's Isles the bird of Fame
Sang the old Baltic Ruler's name.
In ancient battle-days it rang
Like clash of shields, 'mid trumpets' clang.
From Flynderborg—'gainst Viking horde—
And Orekrog,—stout Danesmen poured ;
And Victory hailed, by wave and crag,
The Danish Folk, the Danish Flag.

And of the Baltic's giant Lord,
Proudly its Castle's vaults record.
At Kronborg sits the Warrior-Sprite,
As Northern Champion—Ocean's Knight.
The Hero's lion-sleep profound,
Europa honours by his Sound ;
The World's voice hails, by wave and crag,
The Danish Heart, the Danish Flag.

From slumber, pleased, the warrior wakes,
As seas' deep booming louder breaks.—
He thinks of knightly days gone by,—
He sees the World's ships onward fly,—
Now not for Strife and Slaughter ranked—
For that, th' heroic time be thanked !
Now Friends hail loud from wave and crag,
The Danish Heart, the Danish Flag.

Roll, Stream from Ocean's deepest caves !
Roar through the Sound thy song of waves !
Where pealed, of old the Battle's roar,
Now steam-wheels roll from shore to shore.
Race gives to Race a brother's hand,
And Fire and Genius seas have spanned.
They greet, with peals from wave and crag,
The Danish Folk, the Danish Flag.

TYCHO BRAHE'S FAREWELL.

FROM THE DANISH OF HEIBERG.

The sun sank o'er the grove in night,
  And, by the full-moon's radiance glossed,
  'Twixt Skaania and Zealand's coast
Was Oresund a stream of light.
Uranienborg's high canopy
  Was Heaven's blue vault and starry bow:
  Tycho stood in the moonlit glow,
  And viewed the rounded land below,
With sad regretful memory.

He said, " My native Land ! O tell,
  What is the crime that I have done?
  That thou couldst bear to doom thy son
Far from thy heart away to dwell?

Hadst thou forgot what the World knew,—
  'Twas I should bear thy honour high,
  Up to the stars above the sky?
  The whole of Heaven can testify
That I have been thy son so true!

"Here my Chaldea I have found.
  Ah, ye my Danish plains so dear!
  That showed through the long nights so clear
To every side, the Heavens around!
  My native earth, so low and fair!
  Rather than all the world's rich lands,
  Still must I love thy level strands.
  Most that where the meet Temple stands,
Before the lofty starry choir.

"But yet,—Urania, his Friend—
  Will find thy son another home,
  Which her bright Science shall illume,
And thence to other lands extend.
But darkly yet my path I see,
  Albeit the stars will make it clear;—
  Indifferent to what coast I steer—
  Is not there Heaven everywhere?
And what is needed more for me?"

NOTE.

Tycho Brahe, born at Kundstrup, 1546, of a noble Danish
family, the famous astronomer, astrologer, and chemist,—
though his system was opposed to that of Copernicus,—was
the first nobleman who gave lectures to diffuse a knowledge
of science.   He enjoyed the favour of Frederic II. of Denmark, who gave him the little island of Hveen, between
Zealand and Skaane, where he constructed his famous castle
and observatory, named in honour of Urania, the goddess of
astronomy.   It was furnished with every kind of instrument
and facility for observation of the stars ; and here he received
visits from many royal and other personages who were
interested in astronomy ; James I. of England among others.

Tycho's good fortune ended with the death of Frederic; his
successor, Christian IV., paid him but one visit, and soon the
intrigues of faction obliged him to leave Denmark.   He wrote
to the king imploring his aid, but received a harsh reply ;·
and was invited to Prague by the Emperor Rodolphus, who
offered him choice of three palaces, and a large pension.
Tycho only survived his exile two years, and died at Prague
1601.

URANIENBORG.

FROM THE DANISH OF HEIBERG.

Thou wanderer of the sea !
O, stop thy swift career,
Turn hither to the Island,
My Memory's song to hear.
And let thy Thoughts turn hither,
And check thine anxious mood—
Upon these yellow ridges
A knightly castle stood.

'Twas in the days long vanished,
It shone in splendour bright ;
Now is there scarce remaining
The ruins of its might.
Yet great and lofty was the pile,
In ancient days of pride ;
And grandly o'er the earth it towered,
And looked to every side.

11

'Twas not the hold of Viking,
  By Sea and Islet feared ;
But in Urania's honour
  The lofty pile was reared.
Divided by the sea it lay
  From human fret and jars ;
And ever to the Heavens it looked,
  And to the distant stars.

Firm in the ramparts builded,
  Were gates to East and West ;
And on the North and South, the towers
  With pinnacles were dressed.
High towered the castle's battlements
  Where clustered spires combined ;
And there a golden Pegasus
  Was turned with every wind.

Those wondrous towers, to north and south,
  Upborne on pillars strong ;
With terraces surrounding,
  And pleasant walks along.
And wheresoever one might go,
  On every side the scene
Then looked the mighty Quadrant,
  And the great spheres serene.

And from the Castle o'er the Isle
   All rich the view might be;
With many a grove of lovely green,
   And all the great salt sea.
And then its halls were gorgeous,
   With coloured 'broideries;
And many a garden lay around,
   With fragrant flowers, and trees.

But when the glow of day was quenched,
   And fell the night with dew;
And men began to find the stars
   Through all the heavenly blue;
When, faint and distant, yet the sage
   With ear attuned aright,
Could hear the four great dogs that keep
   Their watch upon the night;

No warlike quest the gentle knight
   Then Fame or Conquest stirred;
Upon the wall he hung away
   His armour and his sword.
And gladly would have fled from earth,
   Its turmoil and its power;
When in his quiet chamber
   He sat at midnight's hour.

And there, through all the night so long,
  He raised his eye to view
The passage of the silent stars,
  The empyrean through.
The stars, that beaconed not his Fame,
  But bore it o'er the sea;
And kingly visitants there came,
  His island guests to be.

But when the starry glory shone
  To other lands afar;
And beckoning Fate had called him forth,
  He came again no more.
And now, but heaps of ruins
  The sad forsaken halls.
Thy house, Urania! now the plough
  May furrow down its walls!

But yet the sun declining, looks
  On Hveen with gracious eyes,
Where paints itself the evening red,
  So full of memories.
The melancholy moon hastes by
  Her well beloved coast;
And Freja's star all radiant smiles,
  With love upon the lost.

Deep in the Borg's foundation
  There moves re-kindling power ;*
It thinks that it remembers
  An olden evening hour.
But for a moment—then is gone—
  For, ah ! It cannot be.
It sinks in Death and Ruins
  The starry Phantasie.

---

* Probably an allusion to a star shining into a well in the
ruined castle's foundation.   .

THE THORN-HEDGE.

FROM THE DANISH OF K. ARENTZEN.

As out in the lovely summer thou'rt going,
　With a sweet surprise thy foot is stayed ;
Along the lane where the thorn-hedge, throwing
　Out its sharp lances with war's parade
Thou lookest, and quickly discerns thine eye
How, winding through thorns undauntedly,
　Lithe and soft, the convolvulus towers,
　With a countless host of fair white flowers
Weaving a crown for the thorns on high.

And from out of the thornbush, thus to thee,
　As of old to Moses, our Lord hath spoke ;
If thy journey beset with thorns should be,—
　If thy life is wounded by adverse stroke,—
Sink not faint hearted, for brake or brier,
But upwards ! by day and by night aspire !
　Like the convolvulus bell-flowers white,
　Threading thy way in the thorns despite,
And smiling, pass o'er them, to regions higher.

JUTLAND.

FROM THE DANISH OF H. C. ANDERSEN.

When Eld was yet but new-born foam on the proud
    waves of Time,
Lay Jutland as a wilderness, with deep black woods
    sublime.
The land was but one forest, where lofty oaks then
    grew,
And strong thick branches twining firm they to each
    other threw.
Then eagles built their nests on high; wolves dug
    their caverns dark ;
And ne'er to Northern Thule then, had glided
    vent'rous bark.
Nor stroke of axe had fallen—and twilight lay
    around,
For ages, ere the Forest first, its human tenants
    found.
There was the home of savage strength; but Nature
    ne'er was lone,
For ever from green branches came some song-bird's
    pleasant tone.

But from the sea a mist arose, so still and keen and
    cold,
It quenched the sunlight o'er the land, as dark and
    drear it rolled.
Then flower and grass and herb were chilled, e'en
    stems of mighty birth ;
And billows rose and battled with the blue-red
    flames of earth.
With howlings plunged the forest beasts affrighted
    in the sea ;
And men, from homes submerged and lost, and
    land, were fain to flee.
The wild wood-fire smote all alike, in one
    destruction vast,—
And all like lava steaming lay.—Then desert ages
    passed.
Again the heath grew high and dark, crowned with
    its violet flowers ;
And lovely, round the eastern coast, stood groves
    in summer hours ;
And flocks of birds, with pleasant song, there came
    and built their nest ;
And human-kind an Eden found, beneath the dark
    hill's crest.
Warriors then roved, and fought and fell ; Home-
    faith its hearth did rear ;
And Bards that taught by Fancy's strains to all the
    Folk were dear.
The King held Council on the heath, convened by
    trumpet's blast ;—

And many a word of power was said, and nights of
 sport there passed.
And generations vanished thus, with many a lofty
 dream,
While sailed the moon, as still as now, o'er Time's
 still changing stream ;
And saw them plant the Cross of Christ, and heard
 the Monks' loud song,
Whilst against Skagen's grey-white Rock broke
 billows loud and strong :
Looked on the proud old knightly days; and on
 their Castle's glee :
And on Niels Ebbesen, who bled that Denmark
 might be free ;
And, pale and round, like Time's great eye, looks
 ever brightly down,
On Jutland's grove-encircled coast, and hills with
 heath o'ergrown ;
On the West Sea in tempests the strong oak's
 branches rending,
While o'er the Hero's Bautastein the flowers of
 Peace are bending.

NOTE.

It was a terrible year that of 1319—no sun, but a heavy
mist over all the earth—at last towards the second spring, the
mist dispersed, the sky again appeared blue, and the pesti-
lence was stayed. But the villages of the centre of the land,
that long expanse of mose (moss) now desolate, called the Ale
Mose, suffered the most. The few inhabitants who escaped
the scourge migrated to the sea coast ; and from that time the
tract has been uninhabited.—*Marryatt's Jutland and the
Danish Isles.*

ZEALAND.

FROM THE DANISH OF INGEMANN.

There lies an isle 'twixt the Sea and the Sound,
 With lakes and woods of green ;
And as sunshine gleams o'er the Baltic's wave,
 O'er the Grove streams golden sheen.

From Kattegat rushes the fresh north breeze,
 With coolness on its wing,
And fair white swans glide over the Belt,
 With the fragrant airs of Spring.

Whispering along goes the Starling's flock,—
 "To the beauteous Isle,—to the Grove's repose !"
" How pleasant in Zealand 'tis to dwell ! "—
 The Nightingale sings to the Rose.

" In Zealand how lovely it is to dwell ! "—
The Lark-choir rings in the sky.
O'er their home in the bending rye they wheel,
Rejoicing like angels on high.

And away, with the birds fly vagrant thoughts,
O'er the dreaming clouds' dim traces ;
Oft they linger o'er moss-grown Council-hills,
And ancient dwelling-places.

And Memory soars o'er the lovely Isles
Which slumber'd in Saga's pages,—
But die not. They wake with song, and tell
Of the deeds of mighty ages.

They speak with the quiet speech of Runes,
From the battle-mound's grey stone ;
Their voice sounds over the bones of the dead,
Like a living spirit's tone.

LANGELAND.

MORNING WANDERING.

FROM THE DANISH OF OEHLENSCHLÄGER.

So sweetly there the holy beechen grove
  Is beckoning me ;
O, Earth ! where never yet the rugged plough
  Hath furrowed thee !
In the dark shade, so friendly, stood a host
  Of wild flowers sweet ;
So cordially they looked to Heaven, and smiled,
  Around my feet.

O'er a wide field to reach the waving grove
  My path was thrown.
There on the sward, surrounded by three hills,
  I saw a cairn of stone.
It stood so venerably, greyly white,—
  In form an oblong ring :—
There, doubtless, in the olden time was held
  A royal Thing.

Upon the Battle-stone there, sat the King,
   With sceptre and with crown :
In sable and in marten robes, and looked
   With father-gladness'down.
And every warrior there, with simple trust,
   And peaceful heart-accord,
Seated himself in quiet round the stone—
   No hand upon his sword.

Upon this hill the kingly castle stood,
   With walls of power.
On that, the lovely maid, his daughter, kept
   Her virgin bower.
And on the third the Temple stood, so famed
   I' th' North of yore ;
Where reeking blood of deer was offered up
   To Asa-Thor.

O, friendly field !—O, stately grove !—
   O, meadow cool and green !
O'er all hath Freja, as a bridal couch,
   Bespread her sheen.
Upon the field are springing, red and blue,
   The corn-flowers tall.
I needs must stop,—I needs must stand and see,
   And greet them all.

Welcome again to the green earth, once more
     The Year's return!
Where pleasantly, in the young Spring, ye grow
     Up with the corn!
As stars ye sparkle, 'mid the yellow flax,
     With red and blue.
O! how enchants me, with a child-like sweet,
     Your summer glow!

Ah, Poet! little dost thou understand.—
     Ah, Gracious Lord!
Thou should'st but see our Master look on us,
     And hear his word.
He never sees us but he calls us Trash,
     In his eye a thorn.
He calls us the infernal Klint,* among
     The blessed corn.

The greatest favour he has shown to us,
     In all our life;
Is when he, sometimes, from his pocket takes
     His folding-knife,
And cuts himself a handful,—good and large,
     With angry talk and clutch;—
And thrusts us, with tobacco mixed, into
     His seal-skin pouch.

* *Klint*—Dan., Corn-cockle; also a cliff on the shore.

He says that in this manner smoked and mixed,
   E'en such poor things as we,
Some small occasion yet the world affords,
   Of use to be.
As for the rest—our beauty—red and blue—
   'Tis useless growth.
His maxim ever is that Usefulness
   Goes through the mouth !

Ye miserable creatures !—the poor man—
   The men so poor !
Who pass through life without one heart-felt joy,
   Of Heaven's best store !
Who never comprehend what God hath made,
   Save only this,—
That Mouth is evermore the nearest gate
   To blessedness !

Ah, little Flower ! as goes with you the world,
   With me it goes !
A simple Poet, like a corn-flower stands,
   And wails his woes.
He is but in the way of the productive corn.
   What fills his days ?
He meekly lifts his childish colour-glance,
   To God in praise !

Come, Flower ! we're kin ! come beauteous darling
    here,—
        Companion mute !
And twine thyself, with magic sympathy,
        Around this lute.
And tremble, as when zephyr moved thy leaf,
        Beneath the harp-strings sway,
So will we gladly sing, whate'er our fate,
        A morning lay.

HOME-LONGING.

FROM THE DANISH OF OEHLENSCHLÄGER.

Wondrous breezes of the Evening!
　Whither beckon ye my Thought?
Cooling gentle flower-scents, tell me
　Whither on the wind ye float?
Go ye over the white strand
To my dear-loved native land!
And will ye, on your waves reveal
All that my heart would here conceal?

Weary Sun! Behind the mountain,
　Flaming red, thou sinkest down:
While in silence and in darkness
　I sit, an alien and alone.
There was no mountain near my home—
Ah, far indeed my footsteps roam!
Nor brings the night sweet slumbers here
As in my Hertha's grove so dear.

Norway's son! I well remember,
  Thou hast said with softened breast,
'Tis in thy native home, thou only
  Canst find the true delight of rest.
Schweitzer! Native of the rock,
These very words thou too hast spoke.
Back to th' accustomed mountains, too,
Thy heart the holy longing drew.

And think ye then that only mountains
  Imprint themselves upon the heart?
Ah! from these naked stones ungenial,
  My gloomy Thought turns with a smart.
Sing ye the Pines, the Firs ye love!
But where is Denmark's Beechen Grove?
And this wan stream which winding flows,
Ne'er lulls my soul to soft repose.

At home there is no river, flowing
  'Twixt narrow banks of clayey hue;—
Life's spring, and Joy's benignant Mother,—
  The Sea—outspreads her silvery blue!
Twining herself with friendly arms
Around her daughter's varied charms,
She soothes herself with flowers to rest
Upon the young Scalunda's breast.*

* Sealand or Zealand is often so varied in the spelling.

But, still! be still! a boat is swinging
  Among the reeds and rushes light;
A girl to her guitar is singing
  Sweet in the silent summer night.
Ah! tones so pure!—a gentle pleasure
Streams through my heart with every measure.
But what is wanting? Tears are springing:
Although she is so sweetly singing.

Ah! that is not the Danish tongue,
  Not the familiar strain and word,
Which in the cottage 'neath the tree
  In joyous hours I oft have heard.
Better, more beautiful—may be;
But ah! 'tis not the same to me.
Better, indeed, she sings, I know,
Yet, pardon that my tears must flow.

Take not my song for aught but this,—
  A sad, involuntary sigh :—
So now, the stream may hurry on;
  Then, seem to loiter gently by.
In many a long-past evening hour
I sat within my own loved bower;
And when my memory backward turns,
For home delights my bosom yearns.

I lost, alas ! my Mother early—
  My early cause of grief and pain ;
Denmark, which is my other Mother—
  Shall I, indeed, e'er see again ?
But weak we are—Life soon is gone,
And Fate is beckoning ever on ;
Yet may I, with my latest breath,
Be locked within her arms in death!

FATHERLAND'S SONG.

FROM THE DANISH OF MADS HANSEN.

Around our Danish field, a fence
  Of billows blue is flung;
And but a little gap therein,
  Where should the gate be hung.
The Danish garden round, our Lord
  Himself hath set a border;
And we will watch it day and night,
  Until the gate's in order.

Within the circle of the sea,
  That wall of waving sheen,
So beauteous Nature is, so fresh,—
  With lakes, and woods of green.
And Nature's stamp,—so frank, so bold,
  So calm,—the people wear;
And warlike, peaceful, high and low,
  Familiar friendship share.

The speech of Danish folk may be,
    Rough as the billows' roar ;
Or, soft as song which nightingales
    From out the green-wood pour.
Or, light as is the west-wind's play,
    Amid the fresh rose-leaves ;
Or, weighty as—within his barn—
    The peasant's golden sheaves.

Well suits the brave old Dannebrog,
    The people's faith and aim ;
The people's Prince, the country's Lord,—
    Their hearts'-allegiance-flame—
Shall never, never be disjoined,
    No more than land and sea,—
Or, song-bird from the beechen grove,
    Or, leaf-bud from the tree.

And the rich heritage we own,
    That will we never lose ;—
Ere strangers on our mind and mode,
    Their fashions shall impose,
We'll give up all, for battle stern,
    Fight, man by man,—a border,
For Freedom, and for Fatherland,
    Until the gate's in order.

SORO.

FROM THE DANISH OF INGEMANN.

Soro ! wreath of lake and grove ;
Cloistered, still retreat !
Isle 'mid heaven-reflecting waves,—
Grove of song-birds sweet.
Learning's home,—Adventure's garden ;*
Of heroes' graves memorial-warden ;
Thou call'st us sweetly back, afar
To days of Valdemar.

---

* Soro is called by Marryatt, "the Eton of Denmark."
The academy is founded on a monastery of the 12th century.
There numbers of royal and illustrious persons have been
educated—Valdemar II. (Atterdag), who died at Vording-
borg, in 1375—was buried in the abbey church—as well as
many other remarkable historical characters. Frederik VI.
interested himself much in the preservation of the sepulchral
and other monuments, and was a great benefactor to the
establishment.

If, in the vale forgetfulness
 O'ergrows the giant's breast ;
If, in a trance affection sinks,
 Is memory's voice represt ?
With soul of mighty ages gone,
Here speak aloud dead walls and stone ;
And Memory's bird, with youthful tongue,
Shall sing its glorious song.

Lakes are sparkling : woods are rustling
 At spring-time in the vales :
Softly heaven's blue mirror ripples,—
 Sing the nightingales.
Learning's cloister-garden blooms,
In peace around our heroes' tombs.
At eve yet Axel's spirit loves
To whisper through the groves.*

When winter spreads o'er waves his ice,
 O'er fields his slumb'rous pall ;
And birds are mute in darkened groves,
 Still is there life in hall.
The bird consumed, with purple wings,
Immortal from its ashes springs ;
And new-born life in winter's hours,
Sounds gaily through the bowers.

* Axel or Absolon, the warrior-Archbishop of Lund, who
rebuilt the Abbey, and was buried there.

Lift up thy voice, undying bird !
 In the high hall, with music rife ;*
And spread, with song, far o'er the vales,
 The kernel-seed of life !
Bring to the days that yet may be
Our lofty fathers' memory,
And to the farthest times proclaim
Our Frederik's honoured name.

* The beech-woods—like the aisles of a cathedral—are often so alluded to in Danish poetry.

FREDERIKSBORG.*

FROM THE DANISH OF HAUCH.

Beautiful Palace ! with fane brightly gleaming,
Ne'er in the north shall thy like meet our view ;
Thy summit so lofty thou stretchest to heaven,
And bathest thy foot in the billows so blue.

Thy Master all kingly, in art too and knowledge,
Hath conjured thee forth, o'er the bright rushing
stream ;
Thy roof over thousands of guests over-arching,
In stone hath imprisoned his loveliest dream.

---

* A most beautiful and unique palace, richly adorned
with royal portraits and antiquarian treasures. Begun by
Frederik II. and added to and finished by his son Christian
IV. It was burned December, 1859, during the visit of
Marryat, who laments pathetically the destruction of such
architectural beauties, and treasures of art. The building has
since been restored, at a cost of £40,000. M. A. Lower
says it is now used as a Military Academy. The noble park
surrounding is the resort of the public.—[*Wayside Notes in
Scandinavia. By Mark Antony Lower. King and Co.
London,* 1874.]

Fair as a rose from the kingdom of fairie ;—
Firm as a word which a hero hath said ;—
Proud as a mountain to day's-light uprising
  Shone thy tower, with the tent of the stars
    overspread.

Peaceful thou stood'st, through our gladness and
  sorrow,
Interpreting deeds of the mighty ones gone ;—
Great as a legend of long-vanished ages,
  In writing mysterious, engraven on stone.

Hardily upward thou soarest, unswerving,
  Stretching thy hundred spires up to the blue ;
And like a high thought which is holy, immortal—
  In the region of calm, ever radiant and new.

Pictures a thousand, and mighty memorials
  Of greatness and splendour, of old time that tell ;
Runes of high power 'gainst the foes of old Denmark :
  Enwreathed by thy beeches, thou keepest them
    well.

  That mighty house is fallen now !
    But shall we that an omen think ?
    Shall Denmark's splendour, honour sink
  In sudden Ruin's overthrow ?

No ! we will die ere that shall be !
  No panic shall our courage bind ;
  In sorrow even, strength we find
To keep the Isles of Denmark free.

THE BROKEN RAY.

FROM THE DANISH OF H. V. KALLUND.

Only great bards thy praises sway,
　　And thou canst not endure the less;
Wilt only list the deathless lay,
Not feeble harpers trembling play.
　　O, fool! hast thou the light's excess,
And would'st exclude the broken ray?

That light by Time may yet be shown;
　　Into a thousand souls may break.
With kindred longing—grief as one—
　　Thousands to laughter, tears may wake,
When Time the scope and power hath shown,
Of humbler bard who gave the tone.

And, yields my song but viewless seed
　To the great summer of the spirit?—
Though fame nor memory be my meed,—
　Like coral insect 'neath the sea,
　I help to build the isle to be,
The world which coming men inherit.

EVENING SONG.

FROM THE DANISH OF OEHLENSCHLÄGER.

How sweet, in summer evening hours,
  When sinks the weary sun to rest,
And song of nightingales is heard
  From out the beech-grove's breast,
To hear the harp's sound, deep and strong,
Blent with the holy evening-song.

O, strike again, the tuneful string,
  Break, pious soul! thy prison wall;
No longer bar th' aspiring bird,
  Within oppressive bounds so small.
But let it in the golden even,
Full of devotion, soar to heaven.

For, oft as sinks the evening red,
   Beyond the wood-crowned height we see,
It speaks unto our soul of Death,
   Of glories of Eternity.
Swell then, my soul! in heavenward flow,
As waves toward sunset's rosy glow.

Strike the sweet strings, thou gentle girl!
   Pour high the thrilling notes along!
And sing, while the last ray departs,
   The last great evening song;
We've sadly sung for friends before;—
Soon to be sung for us once more.

Who knows how near mine end may be?
   How swiftly time goes on with each;
How light and sudden that may fall,
   Which I am wand'ring hence to reach!
Oh, God! for Christ's blood grant to me,
My parting time at peace may be!

Yes! that deep purple, that pure flame—
   Those glowing beams afar which streak,
And redden all the western arch,—
   Unto the dust, of Death they speak;—
Unto the soul, of Heaven above—
That is thy blood—this is thy love!

O, bathe me in thy flames, Great Sun
  Gone down ! and soothe my bosom's woe ;
And in thy shielding arms enfold,
  When Death's cold scythe shall lay me low !
Thy purple blood's atoning power
Sustain my heart at the last hour !

NORTHERN SONG.

FROM THE DANISH OF C. HAUCH.

We have not forgotten,—though ages
   Have fleeted away as in dreams,
How of old, from the North, in its power,
   Life burst in impetuous streams.
Glad witness of heathen-time's valour
   Was Saga,* while watching Time's flood;
And Ocean's wide-wandering billows
   Were tinged with those Warriors' blood.

The dew-drops that sparkle and vanish
   In the forest around Denmark's hall,†
Are the tears of the Elves that are flowing,
   At the thought of those Warriors' fall.

         * Saga, the goddess of History.
            † The beech-woods.

And the hosts of the winds, that are sweeping
From Skania to Dofrefield forth,
Are the sighs which the sad air is heaving,
To the memory of deeds of the North.

The heroes in Death have long slumbered ;
No soul now hath visions so bold ;—
But could we once bring forth such power
As Berserkers wasted of old :
And could we the flame again kindle,
And Dullness and Sloth battle down,—
Where yet could a race be found nobler,
What country could equal our own !

Then endowed with the spirit for Conflict,
As of old with the sword we went forth ;
And ungrudging if Death we encountered,
For that which to Life gives its worth.
And enabled the chill doubts to conquer,
Which weigh down the spirit like lead ;—
Then around the high arch of the North Pole
A light, as of stars, shall be shed.

For, though we by space are divided,
By mountains, and waters, and stone ;
Yet well we perceive that in Spirit,
In Heart and in Will we are one.

In the North shall we all be united,
　When arises the Spirit's new birth ;—·
Then Dissention shall change to Agreement,
　And Wonder shall wake on the Earth.

When that Spirit shall shed down its radiance ;
　When Strength shall recover his sight ;
When Courage, that glowingly burneth,
　Kills not blindly, like flashes of light.
When our Cares and our Jealousies vanish,
　Parted fragments together shall roll,—
Then our People shall wake from their slumber,
　Then our Country becometh a Whole.

NOTE.

The crowns of the Swedes and Goths were united with those of Denmark and Norway in 1389, by Queen Margaret of Denmark, called the Semiramis of the North. Some politicians hope for a restoration, at some time, of Scandinavian unity.

ON MØEN'S ROCK.

FROM THE DANISH OF F. PALUDAN MÜLLER.

Now the evening's Sun declining
  O'er the wood-crowned marge I see ;
With the evening's lamps combining,
Heaven's memorials down are shining—
  The watchers of Eternity.
From high above the eye can follow—
  As seated on the rocky strand,—
Waves on waves with foam encrusted,
  Roaring in against the land.

Whither come those voices sweeping,
  With a tone so deep and strong?
Ah! glad tones are roused from sleeping ;—
All that Ocean's depths are keeping,
  Rolls out in that wondrous song.

As a sigh from the Profound,—
　As the thunder dying breaks ;—
Thus the world's strong voice, in surges
　Through the distant ocean speaks.

Whence come storming here those billows, ·
　With their crests of white o'ercast?
Strong wind, that so swiftly follows—
Covering them with foam in hollows,—
　Tell me where ye rested last?
Billows from the Danish strand,—
　Was it South—or East—or West?
Or have ye pressed the world's great forehead—
　The Northern ice-field to your breast?

Come ye from those Ocean centres,
　Where the world's wrecks hidden lie?
Where lie corpse-like, Man's adventures—
Where the daylight never enters,
　With the darkness there to vie.
Have ye kissed the dead man's mouth,
　Who lies a thousand fathoms deep?
Him whom never morn shall waken
　From his hundred years of sleep!

Flowed ye round proud works which started
   Into life in ages hoar?
Monuments of Strength departed,—
Paragons of Beauty, parted,
   Which the old world proudly bore?
Saw ye all th' abyss hath taken
   And buried in its caverns vast?
Worth far more than aught now left us—
   Worth far more—but that is past!

Yet, at the last great day,—'tis spoken,
   When the mountain sides shall melt,
When the great deep's founts are broken,
And with crash and fearful token—
   Shall be loosed the round world's belt;
Then first from the abyss shall rise
   All that its depths have long concealed,—
Then the world's down-sunken treasure,
   And the dead, the Sea shall yield.

Until then, roll on, unsparing—
   Sea! thou never ending Sea!
With thy strife the storms out-tearing;
The barks upon thy shoulders bearing,
   Till thy depths their grave may be.

Or gently, yet with giant power,
   And freshly as thou first flow'dst forth,
With youthful ardour still enfolding
   Within thy ample arms the earth.

Clear, and blue-green canopy,
   Over the deep's ne'er painted floor !
What can enchain the Thought like thee ?
What power can stir so mightily,
   All depths within the bosom's core ?
Wavering as is the weakest rush,
   Half thine is this world's strength and strife,
Half of Heaven's depth—of midnight's gloom—
   Day's radiance ;—and to both thou'rt Life.

Thou who keep'st the Star of even,
   Within thy skirts,—and morning red ;
Thou who draw'st from distant heaven
Gladly, hues and splendours—given,
   A glory o'er thyself to shed ;
Thou by Heaven and Earth endowed !
   How like the Human breast thou art :—
Ever restless, ever yearning
   For peace within thy heaving heart !

SPRING SONG.

FROM THE DANISH OF MADS HANSEN.

Why should Italian groves so oft,
   In song, as loveliest, be crowned?
Are southern pines more green and soft,
   Than beeches grow by Oresund?
My song of Danish groves shall be,
   Where lilies bloom in clustered knot;
The sparkling wave, the deep blue sea,
   And meadows with forget-me-not.

There is no place in all the earth,
   Beauteous to me as Denmark's strand;
None genial as my native North,
   With summer nights so cool and bland.
Here in my even path I stray,
   And sing, by pleasant thought engrossed;
Here, like the vagrant swan, I fly
   Around my home, from coast to coast.

I love this beauteous flowery wreath,
   Whose passage is the blue sea's wave,—
The beetling cliff—the russet heath,—
   The moss-grown hill, and warrior's grave.
Let others praise the southern lands,—
   My home, my homage here shall stay;
My flight be round the Danish strands,
   My song be of the Danish May.

THE SMITHY OF HELIGOLAND.

FROM THE DANISH OF SCHALDEMOSE.

There stands a smithy on Heligoland,
So lonely it stands by the white sea-strand ;
There Thormod, the smith, with zeal and power,
Wields the great hammer till midnight's hour.
The iron glows red, and the sparks fly white,
With the thundering strokes in the quiet night.

And while thus he stands, to the anvil near,
A strange weird sound comes to his ear :
As the tramp of two mighty steeds might be ;
Yet comes the sound from the stormy sea.
To the door he rushes—looks out with awe,—
And fearful the sight which there he saw.

A lurid cloud, from which lightnings glance,
Hovers wide o'er ocean's dark expanse.
To the shore it comes nearer, and yet more near,
Till at last a horse and a man appear,
Round his head waves the man a sword of flame,
And on four pairs of feet the strange steed came.

Hard seem the sea's great waves, as stone :—
Sparks fly where those dread feet had gone :—
On comes the cloud with its sight of fear ;
Soon sees he the horse and the rider clear.
They are soon at the door—there stops the steed,
And the knight from the saddle lights down with
　　　speed.

One-eyed is he, as the sun-clear day ;
His helmet ice, of silvery gray ;
Around the dread warrior's mail-coat blue,
Bright sparkling stars bestudded show ;
And about his mighty shoulders swings
A screaming Raven, with coal black wings.

"Up, smith !" said the stranger, "and shoe my
　　　horse ;
Ply hammer and tongs, with all thy force !
The shoe is broken—I cannot wait—
Be quick and sure—I am all too late !
Ere Day shall redden the Baltic's side,
A hundred miles I have to ride !"

And the smith his pond'rous hammer swang :
The iron glowed with the anvil's clang ;
Soon the brawny smith did the knight's behest :
To the saddle again sprang the fearful guest.
But ere the next sun sank the waves beneath,
Was the People's fight on Bravalla Heath.

NOTE.

The battle of Bravalla, date 730, is called in the early
history of Denmark, "the most remarkable which was ever
fought in this realm. It was between King Harald Hildetan
and Sigurd, King of Sweden, his sister's son. For seven
years they had prepared themselves ; and it was contested
with great gallantry on both sides. At last Harald fell ; and
the legend says that five kings and 30,000 knights were
reported to have fallen with him, not to mention common
men, of whom nobody knew the names or numbers. It was
not only men who fought there, but also women. The
Schildmaiden Hede, from south Jutland, led Harald's right
wing, and Schildmaiden Visne, from Vend, bore his principal
banner. But on the side of Sigurd fought the renowned
Stœrkodder, who is thought to be a symbolic impersonation
of the Northern Goth. He was a warrior like no other ; and
it is said of him that he had three pairs of arms (a symbol for
the three countries—Denmark, Norway, and Sweden—each
its pair). He lived in three centuries, and filled them all with
adventures, which he himself sung : for he was poet as well
as warrior."—*Nissen's History of Denmark.*

Stœrkodder is the hero of a tragedy of Œhlenschläger,
who represents him as a great and noble old warrior, but

without supernatural gifts ; and in his death, a contemporary
with Hastings, the Danish pirate.

Belonging to the Romance of Danish history, he might
after successful battle, naturally be invested, as in this ballad,
with the attributes of Odin, and held as a personification of
the Hero-God.

This battle is often alluded to in Danish poetry. And we
are told that in the Museum of Northern Antiquities at
Copenhagen are most interesting remains taken from an
artificial mound, under which were found a walled vault, and
close by, an urn filled with what are considered the burnt
bones of a human body, and near, remains of horse-harness,
and some bronze vessels. The character of the remains,
Professor Engelhardt observes, shows them to have been
deposited in the latest period of paganism in Denmark. "We
recall," he says, "the description given in one of our Sagas
of the funeral of Harald Hildetan, who was slain at the battle
of Bravalla about the middle of the eighth century. After
the battle, Sigurd Ring caused search to be made for his
uncle's body, which, when it had been washed and placed on
the funeral car, was carried to the place of interment which
Ring had caused to be prepared. Then his horse was slaughtered and placed in the tumulus, with Ring's saddle upon
him, so that the slain monarch might appear in Valhalla (the
heaven of Scandinavian mythology) properly equipped. Ring
then gave a funeral banquet, and recommended all the grandees
and warriors present to cast into the grave some large rings
and good weapons, in honour of King Harald. After this
was done, the grave was carefully covered up."—*Mark Antony
Lower's Wayside Notes on Scandinavia.*

HOLGER DANSKE.

FROM THE DANISH OF H. C. ANDERSEN.

The Gothic grand old Kronborg stands in the
    moonlight sweet,
While black and foam-clad billows round its
    foundations beat;
Proud ships sail through the curving Sound, in the
    resplendent night,
And yonder blinks a single light, from Helsingborg
    so bright.
The Danish coast stands lovely, with flowery land
    and grove;
And, towering o'er, and black as pitch, the Kullen
    heights above.
At Kronborg now, rings pleasantly so many a
    gamesome word;
A troop of friends is gathered there, around the
    festal board.

Behold the punch-bowls steaming : with song and
    laughter free,
E'en heroes pale, with merriment they cover in
    their glee.
At last the conversation turns—'tis just the midnight
    hour,—
On Holger,—who is said to dwell 'neath Kronborg's
    strongest tower.
" If indeed he dwells among us, 'tis a shame, I do
    declare,
That none, of all us fellows, has visited him there !
But come, let us investigate, and if the Saga's fiction,
We'll call him Poet, who first comes to bring us that
    conviction."
No sooner said than it is done,—the youthful
    advocate,
And all his comrades, eagerly fall into order
    straight.—
Soon rusty hinges loudly creak, torches burn dimly
    red,
Deep in the gloomy passages so desolate and dead.
There every footstep loudly sounds, stones and
    rubbish yonder lie ;
And swarms of shy and ugly bats in frightened
    circles fly.
That ponderous door of iron creaks—now shall
    they quickly learn—
The torches 'gainst the walls they strike—they will
    not clearly burn;

The heavy air cools all around, e'en the hot youthful
    blood,
And again, the blood cools rapidly, Youth's wanton-
    ness of mood.
For in the vaulted chamber, where now they, awe-
    struck, stand,
A vigorous aged man they see,—his cheek rests on
    his hand.
Into the flat stone table his beard hath grown so
    fast,—
His look resembled, otherwise, the Lord's on the
    high mast.
In dreams he strangely murmurs, with emotion
    heaves his form :
" How fares it now with Denmark ?—and doth she
    need my arm ?
Reach me thy hand, young fellow ! See, I offer
    mine to thee,—
By thy hand's pressure I shall know how strong the
    race may be ! "
But with his sleeve the youth was swift the door
    again to turn,
For Holger's mighty hand-grip might bend the iron
    stern.
And still, in dreams he smileth :—"Then 'tis not so
    weak indeed !
And Holger Danske comes to help, in Danger's
    day and need ! "
All silently and pale went forth, from him those
    venturous men,

14

Nor, till they stood 'neath Heaven's bright blue,
    they freely breathed again.
There they behold the radiant stars, and the moon
    so pale and round,
While snow-white waves tumultuous roll, along
    through Oresound.

NOTE.

Holger Danske is perhaps best known in England through the Fairy Tales of H. C. Andersen. In Continental fairy lore he is mixed up with Charlemagne, King Arthur, and other heroes who are reputed to be awaiting a call to activity again. In the North he seems to enjoy a distinct individuality, on which Danish archæology sheds a light.

On an old carved picture of Holger Danske, now in the Museum of Northern Antiquities at Copenhagen, Professor Worsaae says :—"Of all the heroes of Denmark glorified in legends and songs, none is more remarkable than Holger Danske. Who does not know the valiant champion who, though reduced by captivity and want, restored Iceland's, or, as some say, Hungary's Christian King's daughter Gloriant, to her betrothed, King Charles? That he won the victory over Burmand, and slew the grim heathen. And who has not heard of the conflicts of the North under Jutland, in which the formidable attack of the German, Dietrich of Berne, on the domain of Denmark, was successfully repulsed by Holger? For centuries the Danish people have seen in him a living realization of their independence and freedom. The hero of more than a thousand years is not yet dead. Popular belief knows that he sits in the deep vaults under Kronborg Castle, where his venerable beard has grown down through the hard stone table, and where he will sit peacefully till the extremest danger threatens Denmark. Foremost will he then mightily arise, and, as in old times, prepare the way for the enemy's death and destruction.

"It is not singular that the memory of such a popular hero should be preserved, not only in battle-songs, local legends, and chronicle-books, but from time to time in sculptured representations. By the Western Gate of Copenhagen stood, two hundred years ago, a statue in which the thoughtful man believed he recognized his ancient champion. About the same time there was a Burgomaster's Court at Aarhuus, adorned with a gate, on the portal of which Holger Danske, as well as his opponent Burmand, was carved. . Also on many carved objects, from olden to modern days—as on drinking-horns, ale-cans, and powder-horns, it has been the fashion, in Norway, Sweden, and in Iceland, to represent Holger Danske's adventures,—the fame of which, and especially of this combat, extended throughout the Scandinavian North. It is more singular that those really old representations, (though hardly older than the time of the Reformation,) should not have been earlier recognized, of the man in whom the Danish people had for so long a time seen the impress of itself. It is true that the legend of Holger Danske, from its first intro- duction in popular songs, was from the South and West, and that the oldest distinct history of a famous warrior named Holger Danske, or Duke of Denmark, occurs in the following of the Emperor Charlemagne, about the conclusion of the eighth century. But as the legend is evidently developed in the old Danish colony of Normandy, where so many generations from that day have borne the name—le Danois—the Danish, it can hardly be improbable that the legend, perceptibly forming itself, not on one, but on many heroes, originally had its root in Denmark, from whence it was carried by the Northmen to the fruitful soil of France. In all cases the

legend of Holger in the North, whenever it is mentioned by
chroniclers of the fourteenth century, is old enough to have
been forthcoming in the middle ages, though in many different
forms."

The Professor remarks that it would have caused no little
surprise if, in Denmark, his own home,—had now been found
on old church-buildings, representations, apparently faithful,
and preserved from the middle-ages, or those nearest succeed-
ing—of Holger Danske and Burmand; and that it is still
more remarkable to find them on old churches higher up in the
North, as in both Norway and Sweden. The carved portal,
which is the subject of this paper, and of which a plate is
given, was taken a few years ago from an ancient wooden
church in Norway, and affords an instance of the rich inter-
laced carving once so common in both wooden churches and
houses of the better class, in remote antiquity, in all the
North. Norway has preserved the most interesting specimens
in church buildings, recalling in many respects the style
which had prevailed at the conclusion of the pagan era, and
which centuries after, had such influence on carving in
the North, even in Iceland, almost to our own days. The
compartment which represents Holger Danske and Burmand,·
—the former as a knight in complete armour, his sword
piercing through the throat of his adversary, who is represented
as a naked savage or Trold—is said not to be of nearly the
same antiquity as the elaborate surrounding parts, to which it
has been added to make up existing work of twice its age;
being probably, from the style of their weapons, and the inscription, rendered—"hollager dans wan siger af burmand"—
hardly further back than the time of the Reformation. And
this seems to show that, however renowned in popular songs,
people would not, so late as after the introduction of the
Lutheran doctrines in the North, have placed these pictures
as adornments of a church, had such not been an immediate
continuation of an older custom descended from Catholicism.
And with such repeated representations on the churches of

Norway and Sweden, we are involuntarily led to the thought, that this battle must unquestionably from the middle ages, have been regarded, not merely from a traditional, but from an ecclesiastical point of view. It is known how it was sought, in the early days of Christianity, to suit the traditions and representations existing among the people to the Christian doctrines and Holy Chronicles, and, as insensibly as possible, to pave the way for the transition from the old to the new faith. Even in old wooden churches in Norway have been found carvings from the widely renowned Edda Songs. And when it is remembered that the Catholic church had a legend of the Holy George, or St. George, who by killing a Dragon liberated a Christian maiden, how much greater reason might not the dweller in the North have to remember his own earlier champion—Holger Danske, who by killing the foul heathen Trold, delivered a Christian maiden for her affianced lover, Defender of the Faith, King Charlemagne; and thereby became the nearest type of Christianity, which delivered afflicted Humanity as a maiden, from the power of Paganism. And thus from the distant middle ages, Holger Danske may have been regarded not only in Denmark, as especially the representative of the people's Independence and Freedom, but in the whole North, at the same time, as one of the representatives of the victory of Christianity over Heathenism; or of Light and Truth over Distress and Darkness.—*Abridged Translation from a Paper by Professor Worsaae, in the Folks-kalender for Danmark.* 1871. *Copenhagen.*

SŒREN NORDBY.

FROM THE DANISH OF O. C. LUND.

To Brussels Sœren Nordby came,
Exiled, unbent in act and aim ;
Of clear light blue his armour shone,
With great gold dolphins bossed thereon.
'Twas as if plates so strongly wrought,
The tint of Western Seas had caught ;
As told the metal blue that he
Was Admiral of the Baltic Sea.

And brave and reckless,—frank of port,
He came to Charles the Fifth's gay court.
Rich carpets lay on every floor ;
And hose of steel the warriors wore.
Here, free as Eagle's claw is set,
His iron shoe the velvet met ;—
And paced as if on open Val,*
The Baltic Sea's brave Admiral.

* *Val*—the high bluff rocks on the coast of Sweden.

Far o'er the velvet could be seen,
Where'er the hero's foot had been :
The carpet red—where he had paced,
His footsteps white could plain be traced.
That velvet fine the Court, aghast,
Beheld thus cut—down-trod ;—at last,
King Charles in his high palace hall,
Thus stopped the Baltic's Admiral.

"Thou cut'st my velvet with thy foot !—
For that thou, plainly, must make boot.
Great need have I of thy strong steel :—
But, let the foe thy forces feel.
Imprint thy foot on Fields o'erthrown ;
Not thus on velvet, but on stone."
"Yes !"—answered without boast or brawl,
The Baltic's valiant Admiral.

And over Milan's fields of Fame,
The Danish Hero Victor came.
'Mid flowers, upon the stony ground
His marks, mosaic-like, were found.
As once on velvet, here in blood,
The track of his firm footsteps stood :—
Then loud was praised in Kaiser's Hall,
The Baltic Sea's brave Admiral.

Soon Commandant, a staff he bore
With Baltic amber jewelled o'er ;—
It served to soothe the Hero's cares,
At Florence—home of his late years.
There fell, with wounded breast and knee,
'Neath shade of crowning laurel tree,
'Mid roses' showers—at Honour's call,—
The Baltic's famous Admiral.

No mail-clad warrior of the sea
A Brussels carpet knight could be.
On the coast's stones, so rude and red,
There Sœren well knew how to tread ;
And him the North will ne'er forget.
The traces best and deepest set,
Were those that brought to Saga's Hall,*
The Baltic Sea's brave Admiral.

* *Saga*—History.

NOTE.

Admiral Sœren Nordby fought most valiantly against pirates, and conducted himself with equal distinction in the service of Christian II. against the Swedish rebels. At Visbye, in the island of Gulland, he sustained a siege for two months ; and afterwards assembled a considerable force, with which, in the name of the King, then an exile, he took the whole of Shonen and Blegind. When he ultimately found that his efforts did not tend to the permanent advantage of Christian, he emigrated, and entering the service of the Emperor Charles V., died in the siege of Florence.—*Holberg's History of Denmark.*

THE DANISH SOLDIER.

FROM THE DANISH OF H. HERTZ.

On the open field, and when the fight was done,
   Where War's shrill echoes all so late were stirred,
Now came there but a gasp, a booming tone,
   Or tramp of wild steed—riderless—was heard.

And down the evening sank, not with repose ;
   Still traces there of War's foul bloody riot,
Lingered around, discordant—to oppose
   The welcome evening's sad and fitful quiet.

From Flensborg, there was a south Jutland man,
   Standing alone amid the plain so dreary,
And holding yet his leader's steed in rein ;—
   Ah! well indeed might man and horse be weary!

A stalwart fellow—soldier brave,—but sad,
  As fell his eye on mingled dead and dying!
Ah! many who so late were fair and glad,
  Now coldly in their life-blood's stream were lying.

"I thank my God who hath thus kept me sure!
  For space to breathe amid this slaughter dire;
And were it not this thirst 's so hard t' endure,
  Little were left me this day to desire!"

Then looking all around—"Would that to quell
  This stifling heat and thirst, I had but sent me,
A single pot of good old Flensborg ale!
  But here, I trow, with less I may content me."

Yet soon he got, by some chance lucky fall,
  A flask of ale,—and half he sighed in saying,
"The Swedish ale—it is by law, but small,—
  No matter, if it is but thirst-allaying."

Eagerly to his mouth, then, he had brought
  The bottle's neck, and lithely, backward leaning,
When suddenly—upon his ear there smote
  A prayer, a plaint—of urgent, piteous meaning.

A wounded Swede dragoon, he saw aside ;
   Low in the dust where blood was thickly
      scattered,—
Woe was the Danesman's heart when he descried
   How fearfully his foeman's leg was shattered.

"Oh, let me have a drink, to quench my thirst ?"—
   It was the sufferer's husky voice appealing,—
" Here, take it all !"—quick from the Dane out-
      burst—
"Such sight would move a very stone to feeling !"

Then to the parched lips held the bottle near,
   And o'er the wounded soldier lowly bending :—
" Drink, comrade ! ah, sad is thy pain, I fear !
   How goes it ?—Sorely do thy wounds want
      tending !

" Hardly, poor fellow ! drawest thou thy breath ;
   Come, now, let me unloose thy jacket's lacing."—
But with revengeful eye, his brow beneath,
   The Swede kept rigidly upon him gazing.

And seeing thus his foeman stoop across,
   In pain, and hatred agonizing,—
He grasped and sudden fired his pistol, close
   To the brave heart so warmly sympathizing.

But ever Providence for him doth care,
  Who tries his neighbour's sorrows to allay;
So from the Danesman's side into the air,
  The ball glanced swift and harmlessly away.

One moment's space the soldier's heart recoiled—
  "Thou scoundrel! So thou thoughtest to surprise
    me!"
Then felt himself unhurt,—his foeman foiled,—
  And to his knightly post returning—wisely;

He grasped again his flask, in mood restored,
  And leaning up against the charger's breast,
Half of the ale into his helmet poured,
  And offered to the wounded man the rest;

As stooping down and laughing low, he said,—
  "That is thy punishment; now half is mine!
Hadst thou kept quiet—in good faith, instead—
  For thy extremity, the whole was thine!"

So did the gallant swain's revenge o'er-master,
  According as the old tradition tells;
And yet, a Danesman's heart beats doubly faster,
  When he such record finds in Chronicles.

When Denmark's King the story heard, he cited
  The soldier's straightway at his court appearing ;
With glowing heart and royal grace united,
  Thus spoke aloud in all the people's hearing.

"Thy heart, my son ! is noble born,—and I
  Try not to make thee nobler than I found thee ;
Only to bind thee firmer mine ally,
  I wish to hang this golden chain around thee.

And a remembrance of the deed to yield,
  Which of thy high and tender heart hath spoken,
Thou shalt in future bear a Noble's shield,—
  Thy crest—a flask half-filled—a noble token !"

So goes the Saga.   And in Flensborg town
  May yet be found his late posterity.
They prize their simple ancestor's renown,
  And hold in honour high his memory.

NOTE.

This story is related by Marryat—by whom the soldier is
styled "the Sidney of Flensborg,"—in his account of that
town ; as having occurred during the Swedish wars of the
seventeenth century, when the enemy had been worsted.

MONUMENT AND BOUNDARY STONE.

FROM THE DANISH OF MADS HANSEN.

Of victory and honour, only,
The Dane sat dreaming by his hearth ;
By his broad board he deemed himself
One of the strongest of the earth.
Safe lay the lion on the heath ;*
The sword was rusted in its sheath,
And harp's sound called to dance and mirth.

A storm came driving from the south,—
A wall of the house was shattered there ;
In, o'er the ruin swarmed the foe,
And set a boundary with his spear.
The Danes, in fight, strained life and breath :
But many a heart was crushed in death,
And brother torn from brother dear.

* The lion in the arms of Slesvig.

The Dane sits down by his own board,—
    In thought, his hand beneath his cheek ;—
His longing heart for battle yearns,
    But scarce a word he cares to speak.
He rises, and he grasps his harp ;
He makes his sword both bright and sharp,—
    And purpose high his looks bespeak.

But ere he goes to sterner Duty,
    His house and hold to bar and save ;
Awhile with tearful eyes he lingers
    About his fallen comrades' grave.
Unto those heroes he will rear
A stone, which Denmark's maidens dear,
    Shall crown with flowers that Memory crave.

Then turns his glance where brothers, yonder,
    Endure the foreign yoke with pain ;—
He goes for Justice, and for Honour—
    By God's help, comes not home again,
Till he hath set a stone beneath,—
Down there, on Sönder-Jylland's heath,*
    A boundary 'twixt the North and South.

* South Jutland.

SŒBORG.*

FROM THE DANISH OF O. C. LUND.

The storks walk proudly over Sœborg's Moss,
And pyramids of turves the ground emboss,
　　　　　　In black array.
Cheerily still the old flat boat goes past ;
But waters which once filled the lake so vast,
　　　　　　Have sunk away.

Where lifts the thorn its rugged branches high,
Upon the rampart's-mound the red stones lie,
　　　　　　And bleach to pale.
They point the outline round the grassy Toft,
And of the Maiden's-bower and the High-loft,
　　　　　　They keep the tale.

---

* Sœborg—which Marryat calls "The Chateau-fort of
Zealand." Royal personages were often imprisoned there.
It was strong and fair in 1270, when Erik Glipping some-
times visited it.

Now ivy wreathes the prison wall with leaves,
And yellow flowers the torch-weed interweaves,
                    In summer's prime.
Iron and bolts are all consumed with rust ;—
Ground in th' inevitable quern to dust,
                    By ruthless Time.

That Tower shall never more have roof or lead ;
But, now, hath Heaven a rosy cloud o'erspread,
                    For canopy.
And where the captive wailed his woes unheard,
Now comes and sits unscared the vagrant bird,
                    And sleeps so free.

Once warlike engines stood, and ruin wrought,
Where rooted, now, the small forget-me-not
                    Gay clusters flings.
And on the stone where stood of old, the guard,
And sounded battle-call, now sits the bard,
                    In peace, and sings.

The spot enchains his Danish heart and mind ;
He loves the ruins, in and out, to wind,
                    Familiarly.
His thoughts swarm up as bees disquieted,
Upon a board of checquers, white and red,
                    All busily.

Each square is as a coin in Fancy's pile :
He adds, he takes away, adorns the while,
                        In hours alone.
On Memory's groundwork, in the ruin's shade,
His dear-loved Denmark's name, at last, is laid
                        Upon the stone.

'Mid the red runes, o'er all, there shines an hour,
From Hope's green region, and benignant power,
                        Wide and sublime ;
O, Lord of Heaven ! Let thou that radiance stay,
With flowers in every nook and circling bay,
                        In coming time.

THE GRAVE-DIGGER.

FROM THE GERMAN OF N. SIEDEL.

Many a year at Fahrmund's churchyard
   The grey sexton dwelt alone,—
There had buriéd many a stranger,
   And his wife and only son.
Oft he sat absorbed in sadness,
   O'er each fresh grave sighing still :
" Ah ! could I cast off life's burden,
   Now, at age's weary hill !

" Why should I here longer tarry ?
   My hair is white as snow ;
The spade I scarce can carry,—
   My heart is torn with woe ! "
And a spot he long hath chosen,
   Where his last repose shall be,—
A sweet spot all still and verdant,
   'Neath the spreading linden tree.

And he well that spot hath guarded,
  By no stranger dust defiled;
On the right his wife is sleeping,
  And on the left his child.
Once, at night, there came a knocking,
  His chamber to invade;
And a cry—"Arise from slumber!
  A grave must straight be made!

" At the foot of the broad linden,
  That place so still and green;
And the work must be completed,
  Ere the stars withdraw their sheen."
Then taking spade and lantern,
  To the churchyard he is gone;—
As he passes through the wicket,
  The church-tower clock strikes one.

He digs with haste, as growing,
  Both grave and mound attest;
And the labour-sweat is flowing
  From his brow, and cheek, and breast.
Many a tear he weeps in silence,
  Heaves many a painful sigh,
That beside his buried wife and son
  Some stranger dust must lie.

And now, his task is ended,
　While yet the stars are bright;
And he, parting, to his dear ones,
　Says, with yearning fond, "Good night!"
And when, three days thereafter,
　The death-bell tolled once more,
To that grave so deep and silent,
　The aged man they bore.

ALEXANDER YPSILANTI,

AT MUNKACS.

FROM THE GERMAN OF WILHELM MÜLLER.

Alexander Ypsilanti sat in Munkacs lofty tower;
The mouldering lattice shook beneath the tempest's
    angry power;
And, drearily, o'er moon and stars dark heavy
    clouds were flying,—
And—" Alas! for my captivity!" the noble Greek
    was sighing.
He fondly eyed the distant hills, while bright with
    noontide's ray,—
"Would, my beloved Fatherland! that in thy earth
    I lay!"
Then, opening wide the lattice, the desert land to
    view;

Its vales where crows were swarming, and rocks
  where eagles flew.
Again he heaved the sigh—"Doth none of these a
  message bear
From my father's land?"—And then his eye seemed
  heavy with a tear;
Or perchance oppressed with slumber,—for his head
  sank on his hand.
Lo, his face becomes so radiant!—Dreams he of his
  Fatherland?
Thus he sat, until towards him, a heroic form there
  stepped,
And viewed with long, glad, earnest look, the
  troubled man who slept.
"Alexander Ypsilanti, Hail! Be not thy spirit
  bowed!
In the narrow rocky pass where my blood, unsullied,
  flowed—
Where in one grave the ashes of three hundred
  Spartans lie;—
To-day, before the conquering Greeks, barbarian
  armies fly.
My spirit is commanded to bring this word to
  thee,—
Alexander Ypsilanti!—Hellas' glorious land is
  free!"
Then the slumbering prince awoke:—entranced—
  "Leonidas!" he cried;
And he felt his eye and cheek were wet with tears
  of joyful pride.

Hark ! a rushing o'er his head,—and a golden
eagle's flight,—
Through the lattice, as he waved his wings and
vanished in the night.

NOTE.

Alexander Ypsilanti was born 1792, of an illustrious Greek family. He early served in the Russian army, and as an officer of the Imperial Guard, fought in the Franco-Russian wars, and lost his right hand at the battle of Dresden, 1813. In the year 1819, he put himself at the head of a band of Patriots who hoped to attain the freedom of Greece. But after the battle of Dragaschan, 1821, when the hopes of the Hetairai were extinguished, he could only seek his personal safety. He crossed the Austrian frontier, but found himself treated as a prisoner, being confined at first in the fortress of Munkatsch in Hungary, and afterwards in Theresienstadt in Bohemia. At last, Russia obtained his freedom ; but on his way to Verona, where he intended to live, he died at Vienna, 1828.—*From Conversations Lexicon.*

MY WISH.

FROM THE GERMAN OF HERTZLOSSOHN.

I would I were the oak tree there !
  In the green fragrant wood ;
And that my fabric, like the oak,
  A thousand years had stood !

First by the sunbeams kissed each morn,
  While earth in slumber lay ;
The thing which ever, latest shone
  With sunset's golden ray.

Which, every spring-time, green and new,
  Bright birds their home had made ;
While yearly adding ring to ring,
  And casting broader shade.

Still dreaming through the winter time,
   Within so warm and stout ;
My bosom filled with summer tales,
   And vigorous life without.

Waking to tell, with bursting buds,
   Spring's genial empire won ;
Unfolding in each leaf, an eye,
   To bask in Heaven's own sun.

Scarce dreading, for my mighty breast,
   The lightning's fearful power ;
Yet shedding lightnings from my leaves,
   With each refreshing shower.

Slumbering amid the melody
   Of warbling nightingales ;
Illumined by the glow-worm's ray,
   When moonlight's glory fails.

Beholding generations pass,
   And men grow young and old ;
And deeds that seem to throng on deeds,
   With changes manifold.

Past records of the world should stand
   'Graved on my memory's wall ;
For, much which modern men call great,
   The ancients deemed but small.

Wanderers should rest, and children play,
   At noon, beneath my screen ;
And oft I'd breathe to human ears,
   Of that which once hath been.

And when my thousand years were gone,
   And I were old and sere ;
My trunk might form a home for man,
   A cradle, or a bier.

A cradle where new kindled life,
   As a sweet infant lies ;
A board whence, haply, crowned with wine,
   Cheers for the oak might rise.

A house where varied circles meet,
   By good or evil swayed ;—
As pleasure brightens human hearts,
   Or pain and sorrow shade.

In life I'd sympathise with all,
  And when its sorrows close
Would be the pilgrim's final house,
  And guard his last repose.

An oak tree towers before me there,
  Into the sky so blue ;
It softens, yet it glads my heart,
  When its green leaves I view.

THE GRAVE IN BUSENTO.

FROM THE GERMAN OF AUGUST VON PLATEN.

On Busento nightly whisp'ring, by Cosenza hollow
 dirges,—
And in eddies, there re-echoing, come answers from
 the surges ;
As up the stream, and down the stream, shades of
 brave Goths are sweeping,
Who for their country's bravest,—best—for Alaric
 are weeping.
All too early, far from their own land, here they a
 grave must find him,
O'er whose fair shoulders, but so late, youth's bright
 locks flowed behind him.
On Busento's shore they rank themselves, in
 emulation burning,—
Into a channel newly dug, the waters swiftly
 turning.

And far below the emptied depths, the earth they
 hollow deeper ;
And on his steed, in armour full, they sink the
 mighty sleeper.
Then o'er his corpse, his state, his wealth, the earth
 restored upheaping,
For the long water-growths to root, and bind in
 faithful keeping ;—
Turned back again—the stream o'erflowed the signs
 of earth-entombing—
Rushed mightily to their own bed Busento's billows
 foaming.
Then sang the men a chorus—"Sleep !—Sleep ! in
 thy hero glory !
No greed of Rome shall spoil thy grave—no Roman
 know its story !"
With the wild song of warrior-praise from Gothic
 hosts rebounding,—
Roll ! ever roll, Busento waves, from sea to sea
 resounding !"

NOTE.

Alaric remained only five or six days in Rome, and then
led his troops southward, captured Nola and other towns,
and, laden with spoil and treasure, on coming to the straits
of Rhegium, prepared to pass over and make conquest of
Sicily. But a storm shattered his transports, and a premature

death terminated his visions of dominion. To form a grave for the mighty Alaric, the course of the Busentino, a small river which washes the walls of Constanzia was diverted, and his corpse, royally arrayed, was deposited in its bed. The stream was then restored to its original channel; and that the secret of the resting-place of Alaric might never be known, a massacre was made of all the prisoners who had been engaged in the work.—*Keightley.*

The names are left as in the German poem.

APPENDIX.

RELPH.

1712—1743.

The youthful pastor, day by day,
  Who loftier aims and tongues would teach,
With leisure-hand, was first to lay
  The curb of numbers on our speech.

The rugged speech of Cumbria's vales,
  That oft her travelled sons are fain,
When far away, as spells to hear;
  Recalling home and youth again.

He left the grove of classic song
  To roam by lonely dale and fell;
And into strains poetic wove
  Home-scenes and sounds he knew so well.

Or, seated by the brook, o'er-screened,
His summer fancies deftly caught
The hues of rustic life and love,
The tones of native speech and thought.

He died, nor thought of praise or blame ;
For years with grass his grave o'ergrown,
Ere Friendship gave his songs to Fame,
Or reared his monumental stone.

Then where he mused in solemn thought,
Or roved, or sang, both young and old,—
Proud of his pure and simple strains,
And of his faithful pictures—told.

When, haply, many a year had passed,
And many a loving friend gone down,
Strange that some hand should dare assail
His wreath of Pastoral renown !

But Time's strong wind the vapour clears
A hundred years of doubt may cast.
And Wrong his memory more endears ;
His Truth more bright for Error past.

With keener sense of what we owe
To him, who first bestowed regard
On rural life and rustic speech,—
We prize the earliest Cumbrian bard.

1875.

NOTE.

A question by the Secretary of the English Dialect Society, accompanied by a list of local authors, last summer, revealed that there exists a small "Collection of Poems in Cumberland Dialect," of sixteen pages, containing the Pastorals usually known as those of Rev. Josiah Relph. After the title of the first, "Harvest, The Bashful Shepherd," "By the Rev. Mr. Robert Nelson, late of Great Salkeld in Cumberland." The titles of Relph's other two Pastorals are given without any author's name. "Printed by R. Wetherald, Sunderland." No date. This copy had belonged to the late Sir Frederic Madden, who has left with it a note; praising as "equal to the Gentle Shepherd, this Pastoral, which was written about a hundred years ago by this worthy clergyman." He "is sensible that it had before been published, and apprehends that some of the greatest beauties are lost by the alterations and omissions in that edition." There was something startling in the news of a poet's having lived and died there without a sign; without recognition of those around, who, if they had not appreciated him while living, would certainly have spoken of him when dead. As there had been in living memory, a good old minister, Rev. Timothy Nelson, of a Presbyterian family still remaining at Great Salkeld, the idea was suggested of some

mistake, or confusion of MSS., which, like that of Michael
Bruce's "Cuckoo," might yet be rectified : some lack of
honour to the dead, which might yet be atoned for, if, after a
hundred years, the matter could be cleared up. The result
of an effort, for which the time and locality seemed favourable,
suggested the lines on Relph ; which are said to require
explanation.

The question after a little enquiry shrunk into very narrow
limits. The purity of life and simplicity of character of
Relph, as shown in the biographic sketches prefixed to the
various editions of his works, by Southey, Boucher, and
Sanderson, all derived from his friends ; and his early death,
without an effort at publicity for his own writings, preclude
the idea of his misappropriating those of any other person.
Before his death, 130 years ago, he left by will, to a friend,
Mrs. Nicolson of Hawksdale, his Poems, merely expressing a
hope "that the reading them might pass away a leisure hour
of hers, as pleasantly as the writing had done several of his."
Four years after, in 1747, his Poems, edited by his pupil,
Rev. T. Denton, were published at Glasgow. On the other
hand, the prompt and universal disclaimer of all the Nel-
sons who were asked, of any knowledge of the Sunderland
pamphlet, or of any such poems left in their family, was
decisive as to their being unacquainted with, and uninterested
in it. Only one had been named Robert, and he died long
before Relph was born ; and only one was a minister, the
aged gentleman whose death is remembered ; and who must
have been a child, eight years old, when Relph died. There
had been neither rector nor curate of the same name, and
nobody in Great Salkeld had heard of the Sunderland publication, or the poet.

Of the only other person mentioned, and his era, there is
this trace in Garbutt's "History of Sunderland," 1819,
p. 197 : "Rowland Wetherald, Mathematician, departed
this life January 19th, 1791. He was the first who set up
printing in Sunderland. Aged 64. This gentleman was a

native of Great Salkeld, in Cumberland, and settled at
Sunderland as a teacher of the Mathematics about 1762.
Observing the inconvenience under which the gentlemen of
the law, and others, laboured, in having to send all their
handbills to Newcastle to be printed, he commenced the
typographic art; at first in the High Street, and afterwards
in more commodious premises in Maud's Lane, where the
concern was carried on till his death," etc. This date is
verified by the Register of Great Salkeld: "Rowland
Wetherald, baptized, 1727." Also, "Mr. Robert Nelson,
schoolmaster, buried, November 1697."

In the possession of Mr. Jackson, St. Bees, is a book which
furnishes an important link, and on the highest authority.
"The Perpetual Calculator, or Time's Universal Standard.
By Rowland Wetherald. Philomath. Newcastle-on-Tyne.
1760." An Advertisement is printed on the back of the
title-page, that numerous branches of learning connected with
Mathematics, "in all their parts, and according to the latest
discoveries, are carefully taught by the Author, at his resi-
dence, Great Salkeld, near Penrith, Cumberland, where
boarding may be had on easy terms." The book seems to
contain a great deal of scientific information, and of very
abstruse calculation. It is dedicated "To his worthy subscribers (about 120 in number) whose generous subscriptions,
and pressing solicitations, were his only motive for attempting
a work of the kind. He apologises for the delay in its
appearance, which he hopes the pains taken will atone for,
and in part retrieve his character with those who thought he
would never be able to bring it out; so that Phœnix-like, he
may rise from the ashes of ridicule, wing his way through the
ethereal regions, and give them an information of the motions
of the celestial bodies."

It was two years after this, at the age of thirty-five, that
Wetherald, we find, settled in Sunderland as a teacher of
Mathematics. How soon he became a printer, or began to
print books, as he afterwards did, (some of which Bewick

illustrated,) does not appear; neither is there evidence
whether his early years had been chiefly spent at Great
Salkeld; but it is probable, from the majority of his subscribers' names being those of residents in the neighbouring
parishes, that he had been for some time known there as a
teacher, and some of these his pupils.   If so, the name of
Robert Nelson must have been more familiar than those of
his living relatives, for the initials and date are still to be seen
cut in the stone lintel, over the door of the old school, below
those of Bishop Nicolson, who was then Rector of Great
Salkeld and Archdeacon of Carlisle, and "was very instru-
mental in getting the school built, the children having
previously been taught in the chancel of the church." W. N.
                                                          R. N. 1686.
Also the name of Relph must have been familiar, as that
of a statesman's family at a few miles distance; and as,
where printed news was scarce, oral intelligence circulated
freely between villages, the poor young clergyman's decline
and death, at Sebergham, could hardly fail to be known
at Great Salkeld.   In 1747, when his Poems were published, Wetherald was twenty years of age, and with
his reading and intelligence, must have seen and probably
appreciated them.   And for the fifteen years after, until he
finally left Cumberland, must have read, and heard, and
spoken of these Pastorals, like other people, as Relph's.
Moreover, there is internal evidence, not to be mistaken, as
I look over that first edition, in two of the Pastorals, at least,
of locality, where "Carlile" was the accustomed market
town, "Carrock" the overshadowing fell, and "Rosley-fair"
was the prime rural excitement.

So far, dates and probable inferences show the absence of
any claim or interest in the Pastorals adverse to that of Relph;
which is enough for his fame.   Beyond this there is nothing
positive but the name of Wetherald, on that Sunderland sheet,
which is a lamentable fact; and in justice to him, it should
be said, is all that we have learnt really to his prejudice.   We
can perceive that he lived forty or fifty years too soon for the

appreciation of his mathematical teaching in the north ; and respect the energy and versatile ingenuity with which, after struggling hard, he found, and steadily pursued another line of action—though the first was his passion, and probably his forte,—for after death, he is styled, Mathematician. In his early day the tide was strong which used to carry our young men, desirous of better education, by the old classic Grammar-school routine, to Oxford ; the reaction had not set in for mathematical cultivation, by which the stream was afterwards largely turned towards Cambridge ; and at that time, men afterwards famous, as John Slee of Terril, or John Dalton, might not have been successful as teachers.*

It is therefore without regret that the effort is resigned at further elucidation. We can neither know at what time, nor by whom, nor for what motive that mysterious wrong was done, at Wetherald's printing-press—if he did not do it him-self. We cannot see why, if Relph was to be deprived of his Pastorals, and no living person coveted their fame, they should not have been given, as a series—to his shadowy successor : why "Hay-Time," certainly not inferior, should have been separated from "Harvest" : nor surmise what were those alterations and improvements of which Sir F. Madden had evidently been told, unless something to destroy the local fidelity : but which the Dialect Society might ascertain by comparison. We can only vaguely wonder whether for practice in a new art, or for profit, or for love of the old

* In the list of Subscribers to the first edition of Relph's Poems—some-thing less than eight hundred—seventy-five are members of Queen's College alone ; Fellows, M.A.'s, B.A.'s, Taberdars, Commoners, and Students,—beside those of other Colleges in Oxford. To many of these, doubtless, the author had been known at Appleby School ; then in great repute, under Yates. By the rest his memory seems to have been cherished, his themes and strains enjoyed, as only northmen were capable of doing ; and as some of their successors still enjoy a variation of Theocritus, or anything of human and general interest, into broad Cumberland. One hundred and twenty names have the prefix Reverend, but few of Cambridge are given. Over 1000 copies seem to have been at once subscribed for ; which, when it is considered that the public taste also required the time for growth to the more natural standard, may perhaps account for the long time that elapsed between the first and second editions.

dialect, and the old scenes, the Pastorals were thus cheaply put forth : whether the name of good Mr. Robert Nelson was thought a suitable one to pass enquiry at Sunderland, and a safe one as to consequences ; or it had some associations with literature since the old school days—like that of the monk Rowley, over the mind of poor Chatterton. For want of a date, we do not know whether this imposture preceded, or may have been suggested by the exploits and fame of Chatterton. The Rowley Poems appeared in 1769, and he died 1770 : when Wetherald had been eight years in Sunder-land, and most likely before that, had a printing-press. But it was only for his own compositions that the poor boy sought a name of more weight and interest ; his "forgeries," were on a half-mythic name ; and from our point of view, fall far short of the enormity and audacity of a literary "riever," who takes the best portion of a dead poet's long-printed works—casting a shade on his truth, and drags in another real name to cover his crime. For such liberties with the dead, by whomsoever taken, we know neither parallel nor excuse.

It cannot be supposed that those who do such things regard them as so heinous. They know their value as falsehoods of expediency, and expect them to die—after serving their temporary purpose, perhaps without serious harm, when they cease to be supported by other false-hoods,—as they always do. The compiler of that Collec-tion of Cumberland Pastorals knew well that its credit must fail where the first edition of Relph's Poems, with its long list of contemporary names and witnesses was known. And he was right. A copy of that pamphlet cannot now be obtained by advertising, in its own birthplace ; but Relph's Poems, illustrated by Bewick, are in the Public Library of Sunderland. Carlisle, 1798. Mitchell. The name of Wetherald, it seems, is not now heard in either of its old localities. Whether any division of responsibility is indicated by a name mentioned in a late autobiography, in a Penrith paper, I have no means of knowing. "Poor Tom

Wetherell, a job printer, who used to work for Anthony Soulby and others. He died in Penrith, 1809, and was said to have seen better days, and once to have owned property in ships in Sunderland."

It may seem unnecessary to say so much on this subject in Cumberland ; where we have so many editions of Relph's Poems, all containing the same pieces as the original one, there could have been no doubt of the authorship. We do not know that the Sunderland publication ever reached the county : it probably was not intended to do so, and might have been heard of no more, except for the copy which had fallen into the hands of Sir Frederic Madden. But after such comment in print, by an antiquarian authority—as if it had been a correction of some former error, though without date or evidence—it becomes one of those Curiosities of Literature which a mere contradiction is insufficient to suppress. How the story could have arisen, which seems to reflect discredit on one or the other of the names thus put in opposition, is naturally asked ; and it is only for us, who know these circumstances, and the equally honourable names involved, to show that they were only so placed long after death, by some secret hand, and for some unavowed purpose ; and to prevent further question as to who was our first Pastoral Poet.

If we recall the time at which Relph wrote, we shall form a better estimate of his claims to be remembered. He is perhaps best known to the present generation through the Collections of Songs and Ballads of Cumberland edited by Sidney Gilpin ; and there, as I have lately been aware, we hardly realise his distinction from the host of dialect writers who have followed him. He died two years before the Scottish Rebellion, when the country was comparatively a waste as to cultivation and beauty, as we know it, and when literature was as barren of picturesque description, or the interests of rural life. Only Allan Ramsay, of the popular Scottish poets, had then arisen ; and to his "Gentle Shepherd," about twenty years older, the Pastorals have often been

compared.   The Jacobite poetry and music which afterwards
overflowed the Border, were not.   Michael Bruce, who wrote
the "Cuckoo," was born three years after ; and Miss Blamire
four years after Relph's death (in the year in which his Poems
were published) ; Robert Burns twelve years later ; Gray,
Cowper, and Wordsworth, and other poets of nature and
simple life, had not been heard of ; nor Scott, Hogg, and the
numerous writers who on both sides of the Border have
popularized the northern tongue, and rural life and scenery.
From the tinge of classic association and nomenclature in
vogue, and the stiffness of Pope's day, Relph found a happy
escape into the free picturesque country, in his Pastorals ;
which are pure rustic Cumbrian in thought, word, and
imagery.   The dialect is faithfully written, and is a mine of
old association, and of almost forgotten words and customs :
happily without the modern slang, and other introductions,
by which, in some later writers its fidelity seems, to the
dwellers in the *old* country—to be impaired.   His Poems
could never have a wide circulation, as the best of them are
locked up in a dialect somewhat hard for strangers to understand.   They are few in number, and were written at too
early an age to be more than a shadowing forth of what, with
prolonged years, Relph might have done for Cumberland :
but there is the greater reason for his own people to do him
full justice.

G. AND T. COWARD, PRINTERS, CARLISLE.

SECOND EDITION REVISED.

In Three Series. Price 3s. 6d. each, in Cloth binding.

THE SONGS & BALLADS OF CUMBERLAND

AND THE LAKE COUNTRY ; with Biographical
Sketches, Notes, and Glossary.   Illustrated with
Portraits of Miss BLAMIRE and ROBERT ANDERSON.
Edited by SIDNEY GILPIN.

FIRST SERIES contains Ancient Ballads—Cumberland Border
Ballads—Rev. Josiah Relph's Songs—Miss Blamire and Miss
Gilpin's Songs—Miscellaneous.

SECOND SERIES contains Songs and Ballads by Mark Lonsdale—John Stagg—Robert Anderson—John Rayson—William
Wordsworth—Miscellaneous.

THIRD SERIES contains Songs and Ballads by John Wood-
cock Graves—John James Lonsdale—Alexander Craig Gibson
—John Pagen White—John Stanyan Bigg—James Pritchett
Bigg—John Richardson—Peter Burn—William Dickinson—
George Dudson—Miscellaneous.

Cumberland is rich in dialect poetry and in the kind of
literature that is appreciated by an intelligent peasantry. . .
In the three volumes before us, Mr. Gilpin has given proof of
the literary wealth to be found in that romantic region. . .
The interest of some of the ballads is poetical, of others
chiefly local or historical, but not one is undeserving the care
bestowed upon it by the editor.—*Pall Mall Gazette.*

One of the most interesting collections of poetry which have
been lately published. . . We advise the reader to buy the
book, and we feel sure that he, like ourselves, will be thankful
to the editor.— *Westminster Review.*

We cannot recollect a better collection.—*The Reader.*

These Cumberland lyrics—till now scattered—are on the
whole well worth the pains spent on their collection.—*The
Athenæum.*

It is seldom a book compiled on the local principle contains
so much good matter as this collection.--*The Scotsman.*

There is much true and tender poetry in the book, and
much rough, natural vigour.—*Morning Star.*

CARLISLE : G. & T. COWARD.   LONDON : BEMROSE & SONS.

Second Edition.   In Cloth binding, Price 3s. 6d.

THE FOLK-SPEECH OF CUMBERLAND

and some Districts Adjacent; being short Stories and
Rhymes in the Dialects of the West Border Counties.
By ALEX. CRAIG GIBSON, F.S.A.

The tales are remarkable for their spirit and humour. The
poetry, too, is marked by the same characteristics.— *Westminster Review.*

The stories and rhymes have the freshness of nature about
them.—*Contemporary Review.*

Brimful of humour, homely wit and sense, and reflect the
character and life and ways of thought of an honest sturdy
people.—*Spectator.*

The stories, or prose pieces, are wonderfully clever and well
done.—*Saturday Review.*

Small Crown 8vo.   In neat Cloth binding, Price 3s. 6d.

"CUMMERLAND TALK;" being Short Tales
and Rhymes in the Dialect of that County.   By JOHN
RICHARDSON, of Saint John's.

A very good specimen of its class. The ordinary subscriber
to Mudie's would not for a moment dream of ever looking
into it, and yet Mr. Richardson possesses far more ability
than the generality of novelists who are so popular. *Westminster Review.*

Good and pleasant.—*Saturday Review.*

There are both pathos and humour in the various stories
and ballads furnished by Mr. Richardson. We congratulate
Cumberland on having so many able champions and admirers
of her dialect.—*Athenæum.*

CARLISLE: G. & T. COWARD.   LONDON: BEMROSE & SONS

Price 2s. 6d. Small Crown 8vo. In extra Cloth binding.

ENGLISH BORDER BALLADS.

By PETER BURN.

Mr. Burn has already won a wide popularity as a local poet in a most poetical county. The present volume will, we think, extend his fame. It is genuine, and smacks of the soil and dialect.— *Westminster Review.*

A book of unusual excellence, and of real and permanent value.—*Dundee Advertiser.*

The book is an interesting one, and a most creditable contribution to the dialect literature of Cumberland.—*Wigton Advertiser.*

All the best features of the old ballad minstrelsy are cleverly caught.—*Carlisle Journal.*

A little volume of intrinsic merit.— *Whitehaven News.*

North country bards are almost as plentiful as blackberries in autumn. Nevertheless, Mr. Burn must be considered a distinct acquisition, and fully worth the having.—*Kendal Mercury.*

Price 3s. 6d. in Cloth ; or 5s. in Extra Gilt Binding.

POEMS. By PETER BURN.

A NEW AND COMPLETE EDITION.

If Mr. Burn's genius does not soar very high, she leads us into many a charming scene in country and town, and imparts moral truths and homely lessons. In many points our author resembles Cowper, notably in his humour and practical aim. One end of poetry is to give pleasure, and wherever these poems find their way they will both teach and delight.— *Literary World.*

CARLISLE : G. & T. COWARD. LONDON : BEMROSE & SONS.

F. Cap 8vo.   Price 2s.6d., in neat Cloth binding.

MISS BLAMIRE'S SONGS AND POEMS;

together with Songs by her friend Miss GILPIN of
Scaleby Castle.   With Portrait of Miss Blamire.

She was an anomaly in literature. She had far too modest an
opinion of herself; an extreme seldom run into, and sometimes,
as in this case, attended like other extremes with disadvan-
tages. We are inclined, however, to think that if we have
lost a great deal by her ultra-modesty, we have gained something. Without it, it is questionable whether she would have
abandoned herself so entirely to her inclination, and left us
those exquisite lyrics which derive their charms from the
simple, undisguised thoughts which they contain. The char-
acteristic of her poetry is its simplicity. It is the simplicity
of genuine pathos. It enters into all her compositions, and is
perhaps pre-eminent in her Scottish songs.

Carlisle Journal, 1842.

In her songs, whether in pure English, or in the Cumbrian
or Scottish dialect, she is animated, simple, and tender, often
touching a chord which thrills a sympathetic string deep in
the reader's bosom. It may, indeed, be confidently predicted
of several of these lyrics, that they will live with the best
productions of their age, and longer than many that were at
first allowed to rank more highly.—*Chambers' Journal, 1842.*

F. Cap 8vo.   Price 2s., in neat Cloth binding.

ROBERT ANDERSON'S CUMBERLAND ·
BALLADS.

As a pourtrayer of rustic manners—as a relator of homely
incident—as a hander down of ancient customs, and of ways
of life fast wearing or worn out—as an exponent of the
feelings, tastes, habits, and language of the most interesting
class in a most interesting district, and in some other respects,
we hold Anderson to be unequalled, not in Cumberland only,
but in England. As a description of a long, rapid, and varied
succession of scenes—every one a photograph—occurring at a
gathering of country people intent upon enjoying themselves
in their own uncouth roystering fashion, given in rattling,
jingling, regularly irregular rhymes, with a chorus that is of
itself a concentration of uproarious fun and revelry, we have
never read or heard anything like Anderson's "Worton
Wedding."—*Whitehaven Herald.*

CARLISLE: G. & T. COWARD.   LONDON: BEMROSE & SONS.

F. Cap 8vo.   Cloth, Price 2s. 6d.

SONGS AND BALLADS
By JOHN JAMES LONSDALE,
Author of "The Ship Boy's Letter," "Robin's Return," &c.
WITH A BRIEF MEMOIR.

From the *ATHENÆUM*.

Mr. Lonsdale's songs have not only great merit, but they display the very variety of which he himself was sceptical. His first lay, "Minna," might lay claim even to imagination; nevertheless, for completeness and delicacy of execution, we prefer some of his shorter pieces. Of most of these it may be said that they are the dramatic expressions of emotional ideas. In many cases, however, these songs have the robust interest of story, or that of character and picture. When it is borne in mind that by far the greater portion of these lays were written for music, no small praise must be awarded to the poet, not only for the suitability of his themes to his purpose, but for the picturesqueness and fancy with which he has invested them under difficult conditions.

Small Crown 8vo.   Cloth, Price 3s. 6d.

A GLOSSARY OF THE WORDS AND PHRASES

OF FURNESS (North Lancashire), with Illustrative

Quotations, principally from the Old Northern Writers.

By J. P. MORRIS, F.A.S.L.

We are thoroughly pleased with the creditable way in which Mr. Morris has performed his task. We had marked a number of words, the explanation of which struck us as being good and to the point, but space unfortunately fails us. We commend the Furness Glossary to all students of our dialects.—*Westminster Review.*

The collection of words is remarkably good, and Mr. Morris has most wisely and at considerable pains and trouble illustrated them with extracts from old writers.—*The Reliquary Quarterly Review.*

CARLISLE: G. & T. COWARD.   LONDON: BEMROSE & SONS.

www.ingramcontent.com/pod-product-compliance
Lightning Source LLC
Chambersburg PA
CBHW020350030726
47496CB00007B/2088